P9-DFB-118

Good Grief People

There is no right or wrong way to grieve. Each person is individual in their grief and each person expresses it differently. *Good Grief People* has wonderful stories and poems that explore the many facets of grief and can help enlighten readers to understand their own grief. A wonderful book!

Theresa Goldrick

Avid Reader, Book Reviewer, DSW.

Good Grief People is best read before you need it. Honest, very personal stories that "tell it like it is" can help prepare readers for the most shattering experience of their lives.

If they are already in the midst of grieving, the stories won't instantly make the pain go away, but readers can identify with at least one of these writers who actually understands the situation and has travelled through the numbness and pain to the other side.

Patricia Anne Elford,

OCT, B.A., M.Div, Editor, Professional writer and poet, Educator, Clergyperson, Presenter and Facilitator

From Donna Mann's "Foreword" to Glynis Belec's "Introduction" and throughout each writer's contribution towards this book, *Good Grief People* delivers on the promissory nature of its subtitle—Easing the sting of death by recognizing and respecting the individuality of grief and the reality of hope.

My reading, I found, was enhanced by the book's simple organization, which groups the material into parts. This helped me to connect and think and feel with—and to 'journey' alongside—the writer.

Importantly, the first part offers a gentle awakening to the likelihood of the death of someone we love, as well as to our own eventual mortality.

Valuable insights are to be gained here, whether finding one's way through the journey of grief in the loss of spouse, parent or child, or extended family member or friend. The writers bare their emotions at various stages, from anticipatory grief prior to their loved one's decease, through to grieving and coping with the death and eventually finding their way forward in life.

Whereas the writers' faith backgrounds come through as clearly helpful in their journeys, with some allusions to biblical scripture and quotations, *Good Grief People* transcends those, since the universality of grief affects us all. A sprinkling of musings and poetry complement the personal accounts.

This anthology of personal grief journeys should prove beneficial for all ages from young adult and up—for individual readers and couples, and also for group discussion. A potential 'Go-To' book, it may well deserve a place in the libraries and on the office shelves of pastors and chaplains, and as a resource for funeral directors and their clients.

Rev. Peter A. Black (retired)

Columnist, Author

Good Grief People is a marvelous resource for those who are grieving, as well as those who support them. The variety of stories, poems and losses presented in *Good Grief People* reinforces that everyone experiences a different journey towards healing. Time doesn't necessarily heal all wounds, rather, it softens the raw wound to a scar.

Everyone will die. Everyone will grieve. Some will grieve many different losses. What a great feeling it is to know that you are not alone on your journey. How wonderful to hear from the contributing authors about what was helpful, as supports to those dealing with grief. Thank you to everyone who wrote in this book. What a brave and compassionate thing to do for others!

Helen Edwards

Seniors' Health Services Coordinator

GOOD GRIEF People

Easing the sting of death by recognizing
and respecting the individuality of
grief and the reality of hope

Alan Anderson
Glynis M. Belec
Barbara Heagy
Donna Mann
Ruth Smith Meyer
Carolyn Wilker

Good Grief People © 2017

Scriptures marked KJV are taken from the KING JAMES VERSION (KJV): KING JAMES VERSION, public domain.
Scriptures marked NIV are taken from the NEW INTERNATIONAL VERSION (NIV): Scripture taken from THE HOLY BIBLE, NEW INTERNATIONAL VERSION *. Copyright© 1973, 1978, 1984, 2011 by Biblica, Inc.™. Used by permission of Zondervan
Scriptures marked TLB are taken from the THE LIVING BIBLE (TLB): Scripture taken from THE LIVING BIBLE copyright© 1971. Used by permission of Tyndale House Publishers, Inc., Carol Stream, Illinois 60188. All rights reserved.

First Edition.
ISBN: 978-1-988155-05-0 Printed in Canada
Angel Hope Publishing   www.glynisbelec.com
Innovative Print
innovativeprint.ca
Cover Design by Amanda Belec Newton www.tandjstudiosphotography.com
Nature Photography by Wendy L. MacDonald

Library and Archives Canada Cataloguing in Publication
      Good grief people : easing the sting of death by recognizing
and respecting the individuality of grief and the reality of hope / Alan Anderson, Glynis M. Belec, Barbara Heagy, Donna Mann, Ruth Smith Meyer, Carolyn Wilker.
ISBN 978-1-988155-05-0 (softcover)
      1. Grief--Fiction. 2. Death--Fiction. 3. Short stories, Canadian (English).
4. Canadian fiction (English)--21st century. I. Mann, Donna J. (Donna Jean), 1939-,
author II. Belec, Glynis M., 1956-, author III. Anderson, Alan, 1954-, author IV. Heagy, Barbara, author V. Smith Meyer, Ruth, author VI. Wilker, Carolyn, author
PS8323.G75G66 2017   C813'.60803548   C2016-907839-6

This book is dedicated to those
who grieve and to those
whose stories we share

Table of Contents

A Word from the Publisher

When Ruth Smith Meyer and I first chatted on social media, we had no idea that our little exchange would lead to this – a book.

Ruth had recently lost her second husband to cancer and her heart hurt. But she posted something that made me sit up and think. I, too, had been grieving for my younger sister, who died almost to the day, a year earlier. Ruth's words, although I cannot recollect them exactly, were about how she could choose to continue to be devastated by Paul's death or she could work on shifting her focus, reminding herself about the ten beautiful years she had spent with him.

I had told her I was grateful that she had said that and how it had helped me shift from the 'what I don't have now' to the 'what I did have then.' I was able to focus more on the good memories than on the devastation of the loss.

I told Ruth that was a 'good grief' thing to say. Then I said someone should write a book and call it *Good Grief People*. Ruth said, 'Let's do it!"

Somehow it all blossomed from there. Ruth and I talked some more. Meanwhile, another lovely lady saw our initial conversation on social media and soon Barbara Heagy was on the *Good Grief People* team, too. "Sign me up," she said.

Barbara's husband had also died from cancer almost four years earlier, so she understood and she had much to offer to our project.

Then we needed an editor. Carolyn Wilker had been dealing with the loss of a friend and her father was in hospice. When her father died a short time later, the pain was raw but Carolyn was willing to pour words on a page as she walked the road of grief.

And she said she would take on the edits for *Good Grief People*. How grateful we all were, although I wonder if she really knew how much work would be included!

Then we tried to think of someone who had worked extensively with those who grieved. Instantly, The Reverend Donna Mann came to mind. Not only had she experienced some devastating deaths, firsthand, but she had also counselled many through their grief journeys. And she had written many papers and books on the subject. She would be perfect. We were so grateful when she agreed to join the team. We are also thankful that Donna agreed to write the Foreword for *Good Grief People*.

Then we needed one more person. I didn't hesitate for one moment to ask a dear, long-distance friend, Alan Anderson, if he might be interested in joining five women on this project. I have never met Alan face to face but I had certainly met him heart to heart. His social media writings caused me to tune in to the heart of a teacher. Not that he calls himself that. In fact, he calls those around him his teachers. Alan is a Spiritual Health Practitioner for the Fraser Health Authority in British Columbia and works in residential care facilities. He has often spoken about what he has learned from the dying or those who are grieving. Alan helped me many times, too, as I dealt with several deaths in my own family and circle of friends.

So to Ruth, Barbara, Donna, Carolyn and Alan—thank you. Thank you for sharing your stories; for crying as you poured your heart onto the pages of *Good Grief People* and for being vulnerable when it hurt.

Then there is Lisa Elliott. Lisa agreed to write the Afterword for *Good Grief People* and I didn't even have to twist her arm. Her first book, *The Ben Ripple*, is how I first got to really understand Lisa's heart. She is not only a mother who walked the road of grief after the tragic death of her son, she is a soul sister who has taught me much and inspired me to never give up and to trust God no matter what. Thanks, Lisa, for agreeing to write the Afterword. You completed us. And I am looking forward to that weekend retreat with you one day!

To Amanda Newton, my daughter, our graphic designer and 'creator of all things lovely and tech related' on this project—you kept us on the straight and narrow and we love you for that. The cover you created for *Good Grief People* is perfect and everything we had hoped for and more. Beautiful (just like you. Thank you!

Special thanks to our family and friends who were so willing to share their stories. Our hope and prayer is that many who read this book will feel less alone and validated in where they are in their own grief.

"Where, O death, is your victory? Where, O death,
is your sting?"
—1 Corinthians 15:54-55 (NIV

Glynis M. Belec (Angel Hope Publishing

Photo: Barbara Heagy

Foreword

As readers who have experienced the death of someone close, we come to the table as equals in need of healing. We're grieving. We have a broken heart. This is a place where it doesn't matter what education we have, what world travels we've enjoyed, or what accomplishments we've achieved. *Good Grief People* is a book that welcomes you to come as you are, with your memories and grief. We come acknowledging that grief is individual and distinct. Without memories, our grief is slow, and without grief we do not claim our memories in their fullness.

We often hear statements such as, "It hurts too much to remember," or "there's no way I want to think about those days." Both statements are justified; it does hurt too much. However, recovery is achieved when we remember without pain. It is then that we know we've carefully and sensitively cared for ourselves in a way that allows healing to happen.

As *Good Grief People* authors, we offer stories from personal experiences with grief, suffering and death. You may find bits and pieces you can apply to your life to give it meaning and to help move you toward recovery.

The stories recognize the importance of acknowledging this passage of time. Those who suffer, or those who experience loss, offer their gift of understanding of life and death, perhaps serving as mentors, teachers and guides to those who have not yet experienced this part of life.

Without these opportunities, we would not have the rich details and emotions that embrace many of the stories. Sometimes it is difficult to believe how much the human body can endure in sorrow and brokenness. Yet when others have walked these paths with a sense of purpose, we can fall in step. We hope, as a reader, you will as well.

In the darkness of grief, it is comforting to know others have walked down this path before us and that you may find examples of how they managed in some of the stories found in *Good Grief People*.

You may be at different places. You may be just beginning your journey. Perhaps you find yourself on the long stretch in the middle—where darkness surrounds you. Or perhaps your grief journey began a long time ago and now you feel you are understanding it better. Hopefully the stories within the covers of *Good Grief People* will shed light on your particular situation so that you can move ahead.

As you turn these pages, you will be shown many different normal and natural faces of grief. There is no one method or technique—there is nothing colour-coded, no magic words—there are no charts or predictable equations that offer explicit instructions on how to grieve. You will come to the stories from your own experience and identify with some more than others. Your grief is as unique as your heart and soul.

Sadly, death brings a seemingly insurmountable burden of grief at the same time, when logical thinking and important decisions must be made. It is agreed that one needs a clear mind to plan for the funeral and the business that needs to be attended to after a death, but that is not always a given.

Good Grief People will lead you into confident stories showing examples of how the writers managed this in their own lives. Sometimes it can be a tremendous strain trying to find answers to questions that surface while grieving.

In chaplaincy work, I was led into grief recovery training, I discovered I was secondary in conversations with the griever. I learned to "Meet them where they are, and follow them where they go and they will usually come full circle with healing responses." This became my focus. Those who were grieving were the experts in their own process. I was there to listen, discover and find common ground. The griever did the clarifying and the defining. A listening ear was the best gift I could give. For those who are dying, our words can contribute to them having a good death.

This book, through carefully chosen stories, shows how others have managed their grief.

When grieving, an overwhelming question asked by many is, "How can I go on?" Again, *Good Grief People* sensitively frames this question with life-giving responses that initiate energy and hope for tomorrow.

There is never one answer to any question. But, as we have gathered stories that fit our mission and purpose for the book, we are certain they will enable your grieving process in some way. Helping others face the reality of the moment is part of this journey.

We would like to thank those who invited us to join them in their grief. As well, we are grateful for those who encouraged this work. We hope that you, as a reader, will continue along the path of grieving until you can remember without pain. And along with that, welcome the willingness to celebrate your loved one's life in its fullness, in all aspects of life.

The Rev. Dr. Donna Mann

Certified Grief Counsellor (1999)
(Grief Institute of Canada)

PART 1
FACING THE FACT

Away, On or Through [1]
Ruth Smith Meyer

Why do we have so many ways to talk about the ending of life? A person croaked, kicked the bucket, bought the farm, bit the dust, departed, expired, passed away, passed on or passed through—why not say it like it is? They died. Do the many expressions stem from people not willing to face the bald fact that death has taken place or they just can't say the word?

Death is a subject many are uncomfortable talking about. Many would rather not think at all about this inevitable part of life. Perhaps they reason, if you don't think about it or talk about it, maybe it won't happen.

Like the fear of anything, shutting or covering our eyes, running away from what looms over us, only serves to make it more scary and ominous because the trepidation makes the terror grow to unreasonable proportions. Turning around and looking at the reality of death—a guaranteed part of life—talking about it and making arrangements for those parts we can plan, takes the sting out of it and makes it easier to live the rest of life to the full.

Talking about it is one of the best preparations for the time we are confronted with death, whether it happens

---

[1] Originally written for The Word Guild blog/February 12, 2016

suddenly or we are told we ourselves or our loved one has a terminal illness.

More than a year before the death of my first husband, Norman, as part of a Marriage Encounter team, we wrote a presentation on our feelings about the death of our spouse. It was a difficult time, but we laboured on until it was written. We faced a lot of our fears and doubts just by thinking about it, writing our thoughts and feelings, and then sharing them with each other before talking about it at the weekends.

That whole procedure encouraged us to go ahead and make some tentative funeral plans. We talked about the kind of service we'd like, when and where we'd want the burial to take place, who might give tributes, what items we'd like to display to show what was important to us. We even talked to the local funeral director about the kind of casket we'd like to have and inquired whether it would be alright to have the visitation at the church rather than the funeral parlour.

Our children also came to be part of the conversation. At first they reacted like we all do—they didn't want to even think about it much less talk about it. However, we gently encouraged them to give it some thought, and told them where we had filed our ideas so they would know where to look for them should neither of us be here when the plans were needed. We weren't eager for the actuality to occur, but the more we talked about it, the less fearful we became.

We had no idea how soon we would be glad we had done the talking and planning before the reality stared us in the face. Norman was diagnosed with colon cancer about six months later.

For some it may not be death itself, but the dying that makes the thought distressing. Norman, when told he was terminal, said, "I'm not afraid of death; it's the unknown process of dying that makes me anxious."

Our church family and friends became used to hearing our frank conversations about Norman's impending death.

Some were reluctant and almost aghast that we talked so freely, some expressed surprise, but many were touched and heartened at our openness and candour. After his death, I was so relieved that much of the funeral was planned.

As life went on, I became extremely thankful for those whose comfort level was such that they could listen to my expressions of grief and weren't afraid to mention Norman, to talk about him and let me do the same.

I became extremely conscious that there were those who didn't know how, or were afraid, to talk about death. A few times I was quite sure that a person decided to cross the street to avoid meeting me face to face.

At church, I felt the tension every time I mentioned my husband's name. Either there was uncomfortable silence or someone abruptly changed the subject. I became acutely aware of the need for education about death.

When my second love, Paul, and I got married, we knew that one of us would probably have to face the loss of a partner the second time. When he was diagnosed with a very aggressive cancer just two weeks after our marriage, we feared this may happen much sooner than we had hoped. However, God gave me incredible peace, assuring me that I was exactly where he wanted me to be.

In spite of the hours and hours spent in waiting rooms and hospitals, the times of endured pain and waiting for medical attention, the diminishing possibility for activities we had hoped to accomplish, the ten years we were given brought joy and blessings far above what we could have anticipated.

We were free to talk about death, for both of us had already experienced the death of a spouse and we knew for sure that the end of life is as real as the beginning.

Throughout it all, peace and assurance filled us. Even when, at the beginning of January 2016, we were told there was nothing left to fight the cancer and that Paul would now be placed under the charge of the palliative care team, that incredible peace and joy remained. We had ten years!

Having gone through the experience of ushering a second husband into the next life, I've been thinking a lot about the reason society finds so many ways to talk about death. I think it's quite right to surmise that folks find it hard to say someone died.

Being straightforward about that blunt fact is a necessary part of accepting the truth and going on with life. However, thinking about the deaths of my husbands makes me aware of another whole facet of those experiences, at least for those of us who know Jesus as the way, the truth and the life.

Yes, I know both Norman and Paul died, and I'm not afraid or shy to say so. But, somehow, to say they died, is not enough. I was right there in the last moments of their lives and sang both of them from this earthly life into eternity— although this most recent time I had the help of family around me.

"Home!" Norman whispered with joy, in his final moment as I sang, "Lead me gently home." Paul relaxed as we sang, "I can only imagine." As we sang other hymns, a look of pleasure swept over his features. He breathed his last with a smile on his face.

In both instances, it did not seem like death so much as

stepping through the gossamer curtain dividing this earthly life and eternity. They were not so much death scenes as times replete and abounding with life—life abundant.

Precious in the sight of the Lord is the death
of his faithful servants.[2]

[2]   Psalm 116:15 NIV

Lay Me Down[3]
Barbara Heagy

Karen and I met for tea today. She is deeply grieving her beloved husband who died just weeks ago. Every day, after she drops the children off at school, she visits the grave site that's still fresh with dirt and flowers.

"I can't go on. Today I just wanted to lie down right there in the grass and mud and die beside him." She sobbed.

I told her, "It's okay to feel what you are feeling, and think what you are thinking. You have had a great loss. If you wanted to lie down right then and there, then you could have just done it. There's no wrong here. It's okay to meet the grief head-on and yield to it and your feelings. Give yourself permission, the right to grieve as long as you need to and whatever way you need to."

I reached out for her hand and just held her in the quiet between us. I pictured her at that gravesite and what I didn't say out loud is this:

As you're lying there in the dirt, maybe, after a while, you will realize that you're still alive, and it's cold on the ground, and you are hungry, and the kids need to be picked up. And because you are still alive, there are things you must do to keep living. And when you stand up, you will still be sad and filled with grief at the loss of your husband, but you will go on. Not with him walking beside you, but in a new way.

I thought of Cheryl Strayed, the writer, who said, "If it is impossible for you to go on as you were before, so you must go on as you never have."[4]

---

[3] Reprinted with permission from Barbara Heagy's blog entry "Lay Me Down" www.barbaraheagy.com, December 27, 2015. (Revised)
[4] Quote from "Brave Enough" by Cheryl Strayed; Knopf Canada ©2015

"Karen, you know I had my own grieving after the loss of my dear husband. After the initial struggle, I learned to rest, to pause from life for a time. Then every day I got up, prepared myself and went on. Because I was still alive. The Giver and Taker of Life had left me on this planet, so I had to live. I had to live my life for the time I have been given.

Eventually, instead of just moving on, I learned to live with my loss, and fulfill my own life purpose." I paused. "Does a daisy in a field feel guilty when his fellow daisies wither away in the sun and die? All the daisies will die at some point, but since I was still standing after the storm, I assumed I'd better go on blooming in the morning sun.

Because I was still here. So you go on, because you're alive. Because your time isn't up yet. Because you've been given the great gift of more time. Life is precious. It can be taken away in a snap of a finger. I know that now, so I savour every moment and live."

Karen dropped her head down onto the table, hiding her tears. "The sweetness is gone out of my life," she cried.

She wasn't ready yet to hear my words. I know now that I am surrounded by sweetness, the sun beaming down from a blue sky, a child's bubble of laughter, a fragrant flower.

With time, when Karen is ready to look up, she will taste it again. Today she is blinded by grief and the painful reminders that she will never have yesterday's sweetness again. But tomorrow's sweetness is waiting patiently for her—just up ahead.

Today, it was enough to just hold her hand over two cups of warm tea.

———⚹———

Six More Years

Barbara Heagy

As I raised my hand to knock at the apartment door, I heard it—that signature laugh of Paul, my brother-in-law, who could fill a room with his boisterous, hearty guffaw that rang out into all the corners and bounced off the ceiling with its joy. I guess I should say ex-brother-in-law, as my sister and he had separated and divorced more than twenty years before.

"Come in," he called and greeted me with a smile as I stepped into the front hall.

I didn't know exactly what I was expecting, but it certainly wasn't this. I had heard that Paul's colon cancer had made a comeback after a yearly check-up, and that they discovered it had metastasized to the liver. He was declared terminal. The doctor suggested immediate radiation and chemotherapy treatments. He refused it all and asked to be taken off all his medications except for his heart meds and herbal pain relievers. The doctor told him he couldn't do that or he would die—probably within a few weeks.

His daughter, Rebecca, supported her father's wishes. "He said he wants to go off everything." Paul was ready to die if that's what was to be. The other four siblings, were notified and informed of their father's wishes.

Rebecca, a trained paramedic, arranged for compassionate leave from her work and became her dad's main caretaker as they returned to Paul's home and made all the necessary arrangements for a hospital bed, home nursing and personal care.

Paul also made an appointment to have his defibrillator removed. If he died with the unit still in his chest, it would continue to try to resuscitate his dead body.

The nurse asked, "Do you know what you are doing here today?"

Paul nodded his head. "Yes."

"Do you understand why we are doing it?"

"Yes. I'm going to die. I am palliative."

"Is this your choice to have this removed?"

"Yes."

The nurse paused. "I needed to ask you these things."

Paul nodded in acceptance. "I know."

For the next few weeks, Paul's five adult children rallied around their father, helping in whatever way they could as his life was put in order and final arrangements were made.

Rebecca said, "It takes a village to raise a child, and it takes a village to help one die."

David arranged to sell Paul's car, Jordan and Ben made pots of soup and other food to keep the frig and freezer filled. Ruth helped Rebecca with her child's care and relieved Rebecca of some of the home care for their dad. Bit by bit, Paul's life was being brought to a close. Paul's calm acceptance and matter-of-fact attitude was helping them to face their father's terminal diagnosis.

I asked Paul where he got this peaceful acceptance of death.

"You know I was raised on a farm. I've had it from the time I was one or two years of age. I know that death is a part of living. There's no sense to me in worrying about something I can't change."

Paul had already faced some serious health issues in his lifetime, starting with a heart attack at age eighteen. He survived, but when he returned from the hospital that day, his mother was crying and told Paul that the doctors had informed her that he had only five more years unless he had major heart surgery.

Paul shook his head boldly and said, "I'm going to dance on that doctor's grave."

He walked down to join his father and brothers at the barn that day, stepping carefully, step, pause, step, pause. He stopped at the top of the hill leading down to the barn where he could see them struggling with putting up a new fence.

Paul's dad yelled up to him. "How do you feel?"

Paul answered back, "Good."

"Then get over here and help us put up this fence."

Paul's attitude was, "The day before my heart diagnosis, I was one way. Why should that change with a diagnosis? I didn't even hear what the doctor said. I didn't believe it."

That manly defiance kept Paul going. He had a normal life until, once again, he was struck down with a stroke at age 50.

"I figured I was going to die that time, but I didn't. I did the exercises, working out at the gym for one and a half hours a day at least five times a week. I gave it my best and got all my strength back."

Once again, Paul lived a normal life, until the colon cancer made its appearance at age 65. He went through the treatments as suggested and went into remission but when the cancer returned this time, he was ready to accept it.

"I've done the best I could. The treatments weren't working anymore. I am ready to go. I didn't do everything I could do in life, but I did everything I wanted to do."

There seemed no doubt that Paul had a strong positive attitude. I asked him if he had a deep faith.

"No," he replied.

And yet, he seemed to have considered a spiritual approach to life. "You know," he told me, "there are 30 million Americans that believe one thing and 100 Pakistanis that believe another, but they're all sure that when they die they will go to their Maker. Who's right? I look out at all the stars in the sky. Each star is a sun in a giant universe. There are so many possibilities."

I was left with the feeling that he wasn't sure where he was going after he died, but that he was sure he was going somewhere and was ready to accept wherever that was.

I visited Paul again today. It's been over four months since he was given that diagnosis of a few weeks. He was weaker today, but he is still eating, still enjoying his family, and still finding joy and humour in life.

"You know I'm going to live another six years," he told me. He said it with confidence. And then he laughed. That wonderful life-embracing laugh that is uniquely his own.

More than Words

Donna Mann

The day the farm accident happened, my father told me. I didn't understand as I was only a young child, except that there was much sadness about a little girl.

It wasn't long until Mom told me the child had died. I cried, wrapped a blanket around my doll and hugged it. I wondered if Mom had known earlier and hadn't told me. Maybe my dad even knew and had not said anything. I could not fathom what it would be like to be dead.

I worried about being hurt in our farmyard, by the tractor and horses or the ropes and chains. Constant fear troubled me without my knowing what that danger was. Even going to the barn created distress. I could die too.

My mother helped me understand what had happened. It was difficult to realize the truth. She talked about fear and caution that went beyond what I knew about those dangers. My trust in her dispelled my anxiety and quieted my fear of the unknown.

That night, we made cookies.

"Why are we baking at night? You always bake on Saturday morning?"

"Sometimes, our gifts are more important than words."

I didn't understand what she meant, but the tasty cookies took my attention.

After we cleaned up, we sat at the table and mom signed our names on a sympathy card. "Kind words will help."

My parents told me the next day that we were going to our neighbours to pay our respects. That made little sense to me. How do we pay for something we don't have? I didn't want to go, but Mom said it would help.

On our way to the neighbour's farm, I worried about what I would see. My anxiety and fear soon lessened as I stood at the side of the little casket.

"She looks like she's asleep."

"Yes, but we know she's not."

"Everyone is so sad."

"And that's hard for people, but it's good to be sad when you are sad."

I knew this to be true. Somehow this sadness strengthened me to think how others might be feeling. Mom hugged me. Her touch affirmed the peace I felt.

We moved away from the casket and sat with other neighbours. I watched women pass plates of sandwiches.

One of my Sunday school friends reached for a dish filled with our cookies and passed it. Is this what Mom meant when she said gifts were sometimes as important as words? Turning to the man sitting next to me, I offered our gift.

I ate a sandwich and looked around the room. Everything reminded me of church. I relaxed. Groups of flowers stood on a table behind a cross at the side of the casket. The parents wiped their tears as they talked to people, and I knew they loved their little girl. When it was time to go home, they took my hand and thanked me for coming as if knowing it took all my courage. I wanted to give them something, just from me to them, but our cookies were probably gone. I smiled at them—my gift.

Did You Hear Me?

Carolyn Wilker

Icy roads, and threat of snow
but we came
—I had to come—
if only for a moment

At the end of long corridors
behind steel doors and a waiting room
we found you unresponsive
the room as quiet as you
kept company by soft beeping, blinking machines

Though your blood still flowed
and heart still pumped with help
this could be my last goodbye

Not wanting to break the quiet
I whispered your name,
put my hand on your shoulder
Did you hear me?
Did you know I was there?

Only a moment,
that's all we had
then back to waiting
my throat tight
until we left that place

We'd spent so many hours together
shared anniversaries, birthdays,

picnics and school days
even a desk sometimes

That's all it was
just a moment
I knew God was holding your hand.

A Room is Waiting

Carolyn Wilker

I bought the daffodils for my father. He'd been in a hospice for a couple of weeks, no longer able to will his body, or trust his legs, to get out of bed of his own accord. The daffodils would bring a spot of springtime brightness to his room, something he could look at from his bed. I also bought a large bag of peanuts, an item on the wish list at the hospice.

Each patient room had a door and window to the outside so patients could look out, even if they could not physically go there. I'd taken the pot of daffodils and the peanuts and spread some outside to entice squirrels to come closer, so Dad could watch their antics.

I saw a small smile on his face the day I brought the flowers. He liked spring as I did, when the earth came back to life. Other visitors brought flowering plants too, tiny crocuses, tulips and narcissus. They brightened the spacious vanilla-coloured room that already looked like a comfortable place.

My sisters and I agreed that hospice was the best place for Dad for his last days—whether it was days, weeks or even months. No one knew when the last conversation would take place. It felt like standing on the edge of a cliff. We knew the time would come, but would we be ready to say goodbye?

The separation would be the hardest. Maybe Dad was feeling the same way, but he never said anything, at least not to me. He was always more a man of action than speaking, except for certain topics he could really get into, such as trees, farming or care of the environment.

Dad smiled when he saw me, but we didn't talk a lot.

"How are you doing?" I said. After a bit, I asked, "Would

you like to listen to some music?" Volunteers had thoughtfully brought a selection into his room. The CDs were stacked on his bedside table. The news aired on a large screen television and it seemed to take over.

"I want to know what's going on out there," he said, meaning outside the walls of that place, in the world. And so I sat with him quietly and watched the news too, making conversation on stories he commented on. Just spending time together. That day he didn't want to talk about how his body was failing him.

He was surely thinking about his reason for being in hospice, just as I was. I took my cues from the look on his face, if he was tired or just wanted to watch the weather or the program that came next. Perhaps it was facing his death that he was having trouble with. As though the sands of the hourglass were marking his remaining time. I sensed he wanted to prolong his life. He was struggling. It had been a good and long life, and he'd worked hard, spent time with us, then had time to enjoy his retirement. At 90, he knew this was his last place away from where he'd always called home.

Weeks later, when all the flower blooms were done, my sister Mary asked Dad, "What do you want me to do with them?"

He thought about it, as he always did of any request, then he asked her to divide them among the siblings. Mary upended each pot onto newspaper on a table in his room, and for a day or two the drying bulbs made the room smell like the earth, as though it were a nursery where bulbs might be packaged. A smell he was most familiar with as a farmer and planter of seeds and anything that grows in the soil.

Dad said to me the next time I visited, "Take yours home and plant them."

There was a bag for each of us. Mary handed me a paper

bag that bore my name. I had to think where they would go since my flower beds were already full.

"I have an idea where I will plant them, Dad. One of two places."

The next time I came to visit, he asked if I had planted them.

"Not yet. Still deciding."

His face wore a questioning look but he said nothing. Did it mean he wished to hear they're planted? Impatience or disappointment was something he rarely showed in words, but if I could read his expression, did it mean I should get on with it? I would plant them on my return home.

Determined I would find a place, even if it was temporary, I put them in the ground. I'd been waiting for some plants to emerge from the soil so I'd know where the spaces were.

Days after I'd done the planting, I went to visit again, but Dad was unresponsive. I should have done it sooner, but I whispered in his ear, "I planted the bulbs. They're in my front flower bed where I will see them out my kitchen window. Thank you." No reply, but I know he likely heard me; I learned long ago when I worked at a nursing home that the sense of hearing lingers after other functions seem to be gone. Still I wouldn't see him smile, satisfied. Perhaps it didn't matter to him anymore that it was done, but to me, it did.

Our family had the peace of knowing where Dad would go at the end of this earthly life—a whole lot better than here. No need for snow shovels there, or winter coats and mittens. No worries about flowers freezing when another icy blast comes in April.

One day in May, when Dad struggled with his breathing, the nursing staff confirmed he was very close to the end.

They were gentle, always explaining what they needed to

do next, always being respectful of his privacy. More family members showed up and we were prepared to stay as long as necessary. Dad's breathing evened out in the late evening hours, and most of the family members went home—or somewhere else—to sleep.

That next day we returned. We urged Mom to call the pastor. He came and performed a bedside service with children and grandchildren gathered around the bed. The room was full. We hugged each other and shook hands with our pastor. He got a few hugs too. There were many tears as we held Dad's hand or gave him a gentle kiss on the cheek.

"You can let go. We'll be okay, and we'll miss you," I said. "We'll look after Mom."

Only a few hours later, Dad slipped the bonds of this earth, dying peacefully and I wiped that last tear from his eye.

As the philosopher wrote in Ecclesiastes, there's a time for everything, including death. "A time to be born, a time to die, a time to plant and a time to uproot... a time to weep and a time to laugh." [5]

My bulbs are well protected under a garden stone so that no squirrels or other small creatures will uproot them. I'll put the garden stone away for winter soon, then next spring, I'll watch the flowers bloom as they brighten my garden. And when I look at them blooming, I'll remember Dad and his love of the earth, nature and plants that bring beauty and purpose.

---

[5] Ecclesiastes 3:2, 4a NIV

I'm Dying

Barbara Heagy

She waited quietly for him under the shade of the tree. Her beloved husband. Finally, she saw him, walking slowly towards her. He stopped and stood before her.

"I'm dying."

She took his hand. "So am I."

"But you don't understand. I've been told I'm dying."

"So am I."

He shook his head. "You don't get it. I am sick. I am going to die."

"I am not sick. And I am going to die."

He turned and looked her in the eye, taking both hands in his.

"But I have been told that I will die soon."

"I could die soon. A careless left turn may end my life in an unexpected flash."

Pushing her away, he shouted, "The doctors have informed me that it will definitely be soon. There is no hope."

She whispered, "There is always hope. Every sunrise is a ray of hope that pushes back 'soon.'"

He turned from her. "Death is following me like a shadow."

She gently took him by his shoulders and pulled him close into an embrace. "Death casts a shadow behind all of us.

It's the consequence of living in the light. So face forward and look into the light."

He hesitated and slowly turned to face her. His downcast eyes slowly rose to meet hers.

She smiled. "You don't have to walk backwards the rest of your life, staring at the shadow of death."

Once again, she took his hand. "Turn and step forward into the light of each new day. Come with me. We will go as one."

Together, they stepped away from the shade of the tree and walked out into the sunlight.

Jim and Annette

Glynis M Belec

When we received the news about Jim, Gilles and I were devastated. We weren't surprised to hear he had died, but our hearts broke all the same.

It had been barely a year since Jim and his family heard the devastating diagnosis of Amyotrophic Lateral Sclerosis (ALS)[6].

Gilles and Jim had become close and were both part of a men's accountability group. Six amigos who met often for Bible study, prayer, a game of cards and conversation. God had brought this motley crew together for so many reasons. They travelled down the ALS road bravely, sincerely, and most of all, together.

God was their source of strength and hope. Jim's steadfast faith and trust in God's plan for his life was a fierce testimony not only to his accountability partners but also to whomever he encountered during his journey.

Annette, Jim's wife, who is a retired teacher, took a no-nonsense approach to what was happening. She constantly amazed me with her attitude and fortitude in the everyday routines as she cared for Jim, took him to appointments, looked after all his basic needs. She arranged for Gilles to help their son build an accessibility ramp into their home, and so much more. It was obvious she had an unwavering trust in God's plan, too, often reiterating how He was in control and would see them through no matter the outcome.

And He did see them through. It was an agonizing year for the whole family leading up to Jim's death. It was clear

---

[6] Also known as Lou Gehrig's Disease. A progressive neuromuscular disease in which nerve cells die and leave voluntary muscles paralyzed.

that ALS was a death sentence, but it was also very clear that Annette and her three devoted children would never give up caring and loving and depending on God for focus, strength and direction.

Annette wanted to talk about her feelings and share with others how she was coping. She wanted to help those who may be travelling the same path so she spared no words.

"When you live with someone who is failing in health, you need to take responsibility for everything and when he is gone, you just keep going," Annette said. She finds by focusing on the positive and keeping active, she manages well.

"I would not want Jim back the way he was." Annette thinks about how Jim's health declined so rapidly and the suffering and anguish he endured, especially toward the end. She keeps reminding herself that being with the Lord is such a better place. Jim wanted to be with Jesus, so she is glad her husband's prayers were answered, although she misses him terribly.

"Many times I don't feel grief, but when something strikes me, or I start reflecting on what I'm missing, I feel a rush of grief."

These moments of sorrow, that ebb and flow in Annette's day, help her remember what she is going through and usually bring back good memories.

"It [grief] helps me realize that although I sometimes feel guilty for feeling happy, I still have strong feelings about what we shared together."

The ache in her heart remains and sometimes the loneliness is painful, but Annette sees her 'grief moments' as opportunities to give herself a pep talk, pull up her socks, and carry on. Annette misses Jim's companionship and his affirmations.

"Eating alone almost all the time loses its appeal pretty quickly. Having no one tell you that you did a good job cutting the lawn or creating something is a bit of a letdown. Being single at events is not always easy."

Yet she journeys on and doesn't feel sorry for herself. She knows there will be difficult times ahead. But she also knows Who is there for her when those waves come crashing down. And for Annette, there is no greater Comfort.

"What a wonderful God we have—he is the Father of our Lord Jesus Christ, the source of every mercy, and the one who so wonderfully comforts and strengthens us in our hardships and trials. And why does he do this? So that when others are troubled, needing our sympathy and encouragement, we can pass on to them this same help and comfort God has given us. You can be sure that the more we undergo sufferings for Christ, the more he will shower us with his comfort and encouragement."[7]

Gilles and the rest of 'the boys' in the accountability group still meet regularly. It's good for them to do so. Jim would like

---

[7] 2 Corinthians 1:4-7 TLB

that because he was all about fellowship and community. He's still part of their group, in a spiritual sort of way, and hardly a meeting goes by that his name isn't mentioned for one reason or another.

"He was a true friend," Gilles says. "He would stand by me and have my back."

Gilles misses Jim's smile. He also misses his unwavering faith that shone like a beacon even though he was going through the valley of the shadow of death. It was clear to Gilles and the other men in the group, to Annette, his children and anyone else 'looking in' that this mighty man of God with the broken body feared no evil, and he knew the Lord was with him.

Jim was ready to dwell in the house of the Lord, forever.

PART 2
ANTICIPATORY GRIEF

You Can Go Now, Sweetie
Alan Anderson

The following story is my recollection of a couple I met during my time as a pastor a few years ago. They taught me a lot about the love a couple may share with each other right to the end of one's life. I have been honoured to encounter such teachers of life.

Their love was an enduring romance. I remember a time I was visiting with them, listening to their chatter. He said, "I loved her all my life!" She said, "As soon as I learned to love, I loved him!" They looked at each other in such a fond way I wondered if they ever had disagreements. She giggled when he looked at her a certain way and replied,

"Now you stop that!" He continued to look at her and she blushed.

Their love for each other seemed so deep that perhaps that is why they were so welcoming of other people. I knew them well for about five years. They made me feel as if I had always been part of their life and I enjoyed being with them. Perhaps being one of their pastors helped establish our relationship.

Their children were adults and had their own lives. I saw them at times while visiting with their parents. I enjoyed hearing stories their children shared with me. They said that when they were young teenagers other people saw their parents as being crazy in love with each other. From what I saw they were still crazy in love.

She chuckled at how goofy he was, yet in the company of other people he was quite introverted. She was more outgoing and spoke her mind. She'd say outlandish things, such as "When I was younger it seemed all I had to do was look at him and I got pregnant!" That caused him to blush.

When she noticed his blush, she'd gently squeeze his hand and kiss him on the cheek.

While with the family, I noticed how the children resemble their parents in various ways. The two sons were like their father and presented themselves as two even-tempered young men.

It's uncanny how much their daughter was like her mother. When she teased her dad about funny little things, he'd look at her and say, "Now you stop that!" She just had to snicker and reply, "Yes, Daddy, whatever you say!" The family had a close relationship with each other.

My relationship with this couple became dear to me. They taught me many things about the sustaining power of love. He mentioned to me one time that love saw them through many challenges. It also helped them develop a steady marriage and, in turn, gave emotional security to their children. Their later years bore witness to their unbounded love for each other.

Their love would show to others as well when she became ill. He told me their recent appointment with their doctor confirmed the gravity of her illness. He said, as they were walking to their car after the appointment that she turned to him and calmly stated, "This is the beginning of the end, honey!" They both knew they were heading into the difficult part of her journey.

He arranged for hospice care at home, with the intention

that she would die at home. They met with their hospice nurse and had confidence in her caregiving skills A few years before, they had talked with their children about this choice.

If it was possible, they declared that neither of them wanted to die in a hospital. They were both at peace with the decision and their family accepted it. They had now reached the time when their wishes were to be carried out.

During my visits with this couple, I was often moved by the expressions of love they showed to each other, and this moment was no different. Seeing how deeply he loved his wife, I reflected on my love for my wife. I sensed the pain this man felt as though it were my own, as if I was going through this experience myself.

As her illness progressed, I visited them as often as possible. Most of the time, he sat by her bedside and gently assured her she was not alone. I heard him say loving things to her like, "If you go before me, my darling, I won't be far behind you." In turn, she assured him he would be okay and the family would care for him.

As a witness to his expressions of unashamed love, I felt I was on holy ground. I was in the presence of a man pouring out his love for his wife in her final days. Tears welled up in my eyes as I saw him gently cradle her to his chest and pray,

"Please, God, don't take my wife!" A moment later he leaned close to her and softly said in her ear, "You can go now, sweetie, I'll be okay." Tears accompanied his brave words. Her breathing was shallow. He looked at me and said,

"It won't be long now. I feel her slipping away."

He continued to sit by her as she lay dying. He said he wanted to be with her for as long as possible. His emotions were like a roller coaster. He felt a sense of sadness, then a feeling of calm swept over him. He dreaded the thought of her dying yet knew her pain would be over.

With each tick of the clock, time moved on as if everything was well in the world. Everything wasn't well with him. When he spoke, I heard the sadness in his voice. While he stayed by her side, he uttered bittersweet words to himself like, "It will be a relief for her but a heartbreak for me." He stroked her hair and kissed her hands.

The illness that would soon separate them did not diminish the depth of passion they shared. He told me that their wedding vows seemed even more precious now. Their love was a lesson in how tender, although heartbreaking, "until death do us part" can be. Their love would endure to the end.

Tears stung my eyes as I looked at her. She smiled at me. I leaned close to her, held her hand and said, "Thank you for being my friend. I've enjoyed our chats together."

She replied, "I did too. I wish we could have more." She was very weak, yet she slightly squeezed my hand. She smiled again at me. I could still see a hint of mischief in those beautiful eyes. This was my final opportunity to let her know I loved her.

One day one of the sons phoned to tell me that he and his siblings arrived in the late afternoon. It was to be their mother's last day with them. The son informed me that all they wanted was enough time to say goodbye. The children sat with their father as they tried to come to grips with what life might be without her.

I went over to their home early that evening. A couple of hours after supper, the husband sensed his wife's death was near. Thinking or hoping her health would return had become an unattainable dream. He phoned the hospice nurse and asked her to come. Once the nurse arrived, she examined his wife and agreed that she was actively dying.

In the early hours of the next morning, during a beautiful

and gentle family gathering in her bedroom, he heard her final breath as she quietly died. I felt so privileged to be with them as a family. He was holding her hand and leaned over to kiss her. "Sleep well, my darling. When you wake up, you will look into the face of Jesus." The room was peaceful. It was a quiet farewell.

A few months after his wife's death, one of the sons told me the family noticed how much their father missed her. They were all grieving, of course, yet sensed their father was very unhappy. I agreed with the son that the old man was indeed unhappy. He had shared with me previously that he was experiencing what a broken heart feels like. He told me he didn't like living on his own. He said that the house was too lonely without his wife. For the time being, he stayed with one of his children, and the grandkids enjoyed having him there.

One evening when it was time for bed, he said he just wanted to sit and be on his own for a while. In the morning, as the sun shone through the living room window, the family had decided to have breakfast together. Upon entering the living room, they saw him sitting in his chair looking peaceful and with a smile on his face. His eyes were closed and he had stopped breathing. He was with his sweetie again!

Photo: Joanne Wiersma

Those Who Write the Script

Donna Mann

Had I been told as a child that it would be a lifelong challenge to love friends and then say goodbye to them, I might have been afraid of death. However, life on a farm teaches birth, life and death as a natural and normal process.

Although back then, no one used the word grief, I understood my response to death, even before I experienced awareness and knowledge and learned how to express it.

Nancy was my first close friend to die. We were childhood friends. After her diagnosis of cancer just before one Christmas, I visited her at home and in hospital, hoping each time she might feel better. I wanted to share her pain, thinking it would help name my own. Even as she grew weaker and looked more fragile, she took the lead in our conversations, talking about her family. Sitting cross-legged on the side of the bed, I'd listen. Flowers were important to her and I'd often bring a small bouquet, sometimes weeds or grasses, always with a string or ribbon. A jar with fresh water beside her bed each time told me she'd prepared for her simple gift. Through this time, I never felt helpless because she gave me a role to play, and I did it with her help. I was thankful for our years of friendship.

I would be remiss if I didn't mention Maizie. Unlike Nancy, she was not a teenage friend—she was a mentor, a guide, a host and ran a farm with her husband. She was always ready to answer questions from the Bible or the newspaper. From my Mission Band years onward, I noticed that her faith remained strong.

As a young mom, my excuse for knocking on her farmhouse door was always to buy two-dozen eggs, yet I knew we'd end up at the dining room table that was covered with Christian books, magazines and tapes.

Later when she became sick, the family moved her bed to the living room. My reason for coming now was not to buy eggs or look at the books. I sat with her and often read. We talked about our faith and the church. I made a tape with a dozen piano selections of hymns, and I'd sit on the bottom of her bed and we'd sing together. I was too young to know much about grief. I suspect I didn't even understand why Maizie was sick. We'd move past the illness, the pain and the change in our relationship. We spent our time talking, listening and even laughing together.

I had met Shirley while swimming in the Grand River when we were both teenagers. We loved music, sang harmonies, danced, gardened and talked on the phone. Our families adopted children around the same time. We worked together in the church and Sunday school. When she told me her cancer was terminal, I asked how we could spend more time together. Because I lived more than an hour away by this time, the trip gave me thinking time and Mondays became our day together. We talked for hours. I recorded my unpublished manuscript, "A Rare Find," so she could listen to it on her cassette player. Writing prayers and slipping them into homemade cards, and sometimes under her pillow, provided surprise for her. Those visits became holy ground.

Toward the end, she asked if we could 'practise' her funeral service. On the selected night, a friend pushed the wheelchair to the piano, while Shirley pulled her I.V. pole. She invited a couple of close friends, her brother and parents to sit in a semicircle. I accompanied everyone as they sang the hymns she'd chosen for her service.

Another friend read the scriptures, and we discussed Shirley's favourite verse, "I go to prepare a place for you." We helped each other mourn.

And then there was Muriel. We'd travelled in the same circles since we were teenagers and we worked at the Bell Telephone switchboard. After the doctor told her about her tumours, we cried rivers of tears together. She always knew her critical turning points, when she walked closer toward death.

One afternoon, she invited me to visit and have a tea party. Her daughter had prepared egg salad sandwiches, sweet pickles and strong coffee. I always tried to follow Muriel's lead. She led the discussion and never avoided difficult issues of death. It appeared to me that she wanted to let go of life and that often became a familiar topic. The last time I saw her, she didn't want to talk. This did not offend me as she wanted to be quiet. Perhaps she was readying herself for the next step of her journey.

One friend, Bev, laughed at the same jokes that I did, talked about difficult topics, and many people said we looked like sisters. She and I were 'number-please' girls, too. We had a lifetime of friendship. She had known for a while of her stage 4 cancer before she told me. When we talked, I remember thinking I do not want to believe this. I do not want to hear this. Maybe I even said it.

We both talked through our tears. She insisted that I understand her condition and her life expectancy. We had plenty of work to do before the end. We used our time well—talked on the phone, wrote notes and visited. The most precious for me was spending time together sitting and talking. She knew what she wanted to say, and she trusted me not to interrupt, not necessarily agree, but to just listen. I spoke, as a friend, at her funeral and read a verse of the country song, "A Daisy a Day" by Jud Strunk, which suggests relationships continue in a different way. Sometimes, we say to others what we need to hear ourselves. As a result, I often put a daisy in the flower bowl to remember her.

Now, so many years after my friends died, I remember them when I drive by their earlier residences. I think about each one and wonder what we'd be doing together if they had lived.

In my friends' illnesses, and when one would think they had nothing to offer to life, they became teachers for anybody, open to learning. They were the experts. They exemplified how to share deep friendship and walk together as they surrendered to death. Every one of my friends watched me yield to mourning. When I cried in their presence, not one of them said, "Don't cry." They were mentors, leading me along this treacherous journey, and giving me space to mourn with them was their last gift to me.

I Will Never Be the Same[8]

Barbara Heagy

I woke early this morning and my eyes slowly adjusted to dawn's early light filtering in through the bedroom curtains. I rolled over in bed. Tom, my darling hubby, was still asleep. His cancer and its treatments were leaving him exhausted and he was sleeping for longer stretches of time.

I sat up and grabbed my journal and a pen. It was time to do a serious assessment and write down my feelings about the last few months since cancer reared its monstrous head in our lives. Journaling seems to help me put things in perspective with order and insight.

Pen in hand, I wrote:

Let's sum up this experience and its effect on our lives over the last three months. So far on this cancer journey, Tom has been able to take care of most of his needs and hold his own.

The first stage, including the brain surgery, meant a short stay in the hospital. He was determined he was going to go home as quickly as possible, and two and a half days later, the hospital discharged him.

The next stage was radiation which, once again, Tom found not too bad, not too taxing on his energy. The month after the radiation he found himself more tired than usual, probably working at about 50 percent of his capacity, but he walked daily, as long as he took frequent rests. He was able to complete light household chores such as cooking, dishes, and laundry. A mix-up in medication for his lung condition drained his energy during this time, but he seemed to

---

[8] An excerpt from Barbara Heagy's self-published book 10 – A Story of Love, Life, and Loss. Reprinted with permission. Revised.

recuperate, although I would say not to his original status.

Three weeks of radiation treatments ended and one month later chemotherapy treatments began. Tom found the boost from the drugs he received significantly lifted his energy levels. The day after his first session of three treatments, he volunteered at the Hillside Music Festival as we do every year, and we camped on Guelph Island for four days. The day he got back from Hillside, his body seemed to collapse. He slept for twenty-seven hours only rising to use the bathroom. For the next few weeks, he would wake and arise only for an hour or two at a time, barely eating anything.

Late summer, when Tom returned to the hospital for his second chemotherapy session, blood tests showed a serious drop in white blood cell counts. His body weight had dropped ten pounds. The oncologist cancelled his treatment, changed his chemotherapy drug to try and find one that would not leave him nauseous, and prescribed another daily drug to combat heartburn and gastric reflux.

A home care nurse consultation was suggested for weekly nursing care and diet advice and monitoring. At our first meeting, she quickly reassured me, "Not that you're doing a poor job taking care of him."

I was agreeable to her suggestions and said, "He won't listen to me when I tell him to get up or eat. Maybe he will listen to a professional."

Tom and I had a serious sit-down after receiving the news of the cancelled chemo treatment. I talked, he listened.

"In the past, you tended to just retreat into your own little world in the face of trials and tribulations. You turn off your cell phone, lock your door, and just withdraw from the world. That's what you have tried to do with this cancer, but it's not going to work. You have to fight cancer. You have to stand up to it, be angry, and say, 'I refuse to be dominated by this.'

You have to make yourself get up every day, even when every bone in your body is saying, just lie here. You'll be okay if you only rest. You have to walk, even if it's the short distance to the end of the driveway and back. You have to eat, even when you have absolutely no desire to eat anything.

Cancer demands a fight and you have to become a fighter. Because if you don't, you will be too weak to take your chemo treatments, and if you don't take your treatments, you will die."

Something, somewhere touched a chord in Tom because I found him sitting up just a little bit straighter. He began to stay awake for more extended periods of time and, although the quantities were very small, he tried to eat something once or twice a day.

I hope that things continue to improve this week, and next Tuesday, when he goes back for another blood test, he can resume his chemotherapy treatments.

The treatment has had its effect on me too. As Tom has withdrawn from me, sleeping for long periods, I have been alone much of the time. There's been a certain level of anxiety, and I find myself regularly checking him to ensure that he is okay. In the back of my mind is my father on the day he died. He, too, told Jan, "I'm tired. I think I'll just stay in bed for a while longer." And it was a horrifying shock to her to find him dead when she checked on him later that morning.

I find myself standing over Tom, listening for breathing and checking the covers for signs of subtle movement. At night in bed, when I wake in the middle of the night, I touch his body. Is he still warm? There is nothing more reassuring than feeling his soft, warm body next to mine.

With Tom's sickness, his senses have become extremely heightened—smells bother him, including mine. He turns away from me if I eat too much garlic or other spicy foods. His hearing is sensitive, "Lower your voice, please." His taste has changed; he wants only the blandest and simplest of foods, chosen from the most limited variety, and even this can change with one mouthful. He asks for pork and beans and then eats only two teaspoons and tires of it. His sense of touch is acute. He recoils and cringes from me, sometimes with even the lightest touch.

At Hillside, he told a little girl who was crawling onto his lap, "Please don't touch me."

Physical intimacy is non-existent and even gentle cuddling is rare. Kisses, too, have become painful as the chemotherapy has caused sores on his lips. Conversation, when he has been awake and sitting up, is quiet and limited. He has withdrawn from me in so many ways that I have often felt lonely, as if I have lost him already. With that comes deep sadness. I just want my Tom back and I am scared it won't happen. Even if he survives this, I fear he will be a changed man. Even he fears that. Last night he made a comment about never being the same again.

I am beginning to see Tom in a new way. We are moving from a husband and wife, equal-members-of-the-house role, to patient and caretaker. He's been sick enough the last few weeks that I have had to see him as a patient, giving him the same level of care I would to a small child. That hasn't included toilet and bathing assistance, but it may come to that. I have been his beck-and-call girl, making coffee, getting glasses of water or a box of Kleenex, and driving him even the shortest distances.

I have had to take on his household duties, and I now do all the cooking, dishes, housework, grass cutting, gardening, most of the laundry, and garbage detail. This is a new place for me and a place that, up until now, both Tom and I have been denying as we refuse to accept the cancer and its effect on his body. As time moves on and Tom's condition changes, we do too.

I'm not sure I will be able to stay with my full-time teaching job once school gets underway. The doctors have told us there is no cure for this. All they can do is try and control it. The statistics on small-cell lung cancer are not good. From what I've read, only two percent of patients are still alive after five years. A friend at work said, "Maybe he will be the two percent" and there is nothing more I would hope for. But I also have to accept that maybe he won't. All we may be given is some more time.

A book I purchased, *The Cleveland Clinic Guide to Lung Cancer*, emphasized that for most patients, current treatments do not cure the cancer and most patients, even those who respond well to treatment, will relapse, sometimes within a few months of treatment. I have not shared this information with Tom. He doesn't want to hear any negative talk.

Things, however, do look very serious, and a true miracle from God is needed. But, I do believe in miracles, and I do believe that God is walking this journey with us, no matter what happens. I have had my own private conversations with God and I have asked for more quality time with Tom. Asked for it in the way a daughter asks her parent for a favour or request. Asked knowing that it may be granted simply because I am a valued, loved child of God and deserve it for no other reason than that.

So I stay positive and open to miracles. Every day when I wake up, I thank God for the promise of a new day together, and every night when I go to sleep, I say a prayer of gratefulness for the extra time given. I pray for continued hope and strength on this journey. If for some reason God sees fit to take Tom earlier rather than later, I trust that all is as it should be.

Do I like it? Not one little bit.

Journey Toward Death[9]

Ruth Smith-Meyer

Never will I forget the call that came that March morning. Could my husband and I to come to the doctor's office to get the results of the colonoscopy Norman had a week before? The very fact that they didn't give us an 'all clear' over the phone implanted a distinct feeling that the news was not good. It wasn't. A tumour in his colon was advanced enough that they weren't sure whether it had already moved through the lining. An appointment was immediately scheduled with a surgeon, because Norman would require surgery.

After the initial news of cancer, we sat on the couch with our arms around each other, sharing the feelings that raged through us. Then Norman spoke in his usual calm manner, "Ruth, the hardest times in our lives have been the times we have grown the most, both as persons and in our love and understanding of each other. Let's see how we can grow and what we can learn from this time." To that, we committed ourselves.

Norman asked to be anointed with oil the evening before his operation. Friends, acquaintances, and their churches were praying for healing for Norman. We were entirely convinced that God could and would heal.

The March surgery went well and he made a quick recovery. Norman returned to much of his usual routine. Life seemed much more tenuous than before, but we praised God for the positive indications of health.

We made a list of things we would still like to do together.

---

[9] Adapted from Out of the Ordinary, Ruth Smith Meyer, Word Alive Press, 2015

We continued our involvement in the church and our usual commitments as we could.

We took walks in the woods, drives to favourite spots, prayed in most of those places, and always shared our thoughts and feelings. These were sacred days of togetherness, enhanced by the fact that, because of a Marriage Encounter weekend, our relationship had grown to a depth that allowed full disclosure of our emotions to one another.

Spots on Norman's liver had shown up on a CAT scan just before his surgery. During the operation, the surgeon examined his liver and couldn't detect anything. Even though subsequent biopsies of the liver showed no signs of cancer, the doctors thought removing the effected lobe, just in case, would give him the best chance.

We felt some reluctance to spoil what seemed to be a good recovery by undergoing such an extensive operation. We prayed much about it and felt God was indicating to go this route. We were assured that God was in control. In fact, Norman said in the car, on his way in to the hospital for surgery, that he felt like the healed leper going to show himself to the priest.

It was to be six-to-eight-hour surgery that June morning. When the doctor came to the waiting room after only two hours, he didn't have to say a word to send our hearts plunging downward. Both lobes of the liver were involved.

There was nothing they could do. He said it would take at least an hour before Norman woke up, but then we could see him in his room.

With aching hearts, we called the rest of the family who had planned to come before the end of the surgery. One of the chaplains at the hospital was a personal friend, and so my daughter and I went to see him. He listened and prayed with us. I asked how he thought I should break the news to Norman that the surgery didn't accomplish what we had hoped.

"Ruth, I know the relationship you and Norman have. The truth is the only option you have. You need to tell him if he asks."

The first question Norman asked was, "What time is it?" When I told him, he said, "That's not near as long as they said it would take. Does that mean good news or bad?"

"My darling, they couldn't do anything because both lobes of your liver were filled with cancer."

"So how long do I have?"

"The doctor said no one knows for sure, but he thought nine months to a year."

He drifted back to sleep.

Even more, now, our hope was that God would still bring healing. So many of our friends, from every era and area of our lives, committed themselves to pray.

On the way home from the hospital, Norman said, "Let's look after our business affairs, talk about how you would manage alone, plan my funeral, then concentrate on living fully each moment we are given, whether that be months or years." I took a six-month leave of absence from my work and we began.

That meant facing the possibilities head-on, but it also meant doing it together. It was a literal expression of total reliance on God, and faith in the One who first loved us.

Allowing our immediate, extended and church family and friends to walk with us in our journey seemed a natural extension of openly sharing our experiences. The benefits were not ours alone. Many people, although some felt uncomfortable at first, were affirmative of our candour. Our children's co-workers expressed amazement at that openness, yet, in the process, they were able to talk about their feelings and fears and hopes.

The more we shared, the more open we became, the more comfortable with being honest with ourselves, each other and those around us.

One of our banners at Marriage Encounter states "Henceforth there shall be such closeness that when one weeps the other tastes salt." The truth of that statement was amplified in those months to come.

After the second surgery, Norman had been doing some walking, reading and easy activities, trying to regain his strength. One evening after an early supper, Norman went to lie on the couch. He had slept a lot that day. I became aware of the taste of salt.

I asked if he was sleeping because he was tired, or to escape his thoughts. He acknowledged that perhaps it was the latter. I suggested a drive to see the grove of nut trees he had planted on our farm. He agreed. We spent a beautiful two hours talking about our feelings, the distinct possibility of the limited time we had left, the implications for me and for our family.

He felt deep distress at leaving me alone so soon. He also shared his grief at leaving the children and grandchildren at this stage in their lives. I suggested that he might like to write a love letter to each of them—something tangible they could keep and read often.

This appealed to him right away. He began the next morning and by summer's end, had written to each of the children, the in-laws and grandchildren. Those letters are something they will treasure for the rest of their lives.

At one point, having seen his health rapidly deteriorate, I had a day that I felt sheer panic at being left alone. Norman tasted salt. He gently probed my thoughts and encouraged me to share.

He listened until I had spilled all my fears and self-doubt. He just held me until I was resting in his love and care, then quietly he told me of the strength that he saw in me, reminded me of things I could do without him, and that I would not be alone. He told me that our family and friends would be supportive, and God, who had walked with me throughout my life, would not forsake me.

Up until the week Noman died, even sometimes when I thought he was semi-conscious, he would suddenly call my name. When I responded, he would tell me some other reason he believed in my ability to continue, or something else I could still accomplish.

In the last weeks of his life, many people came to kneel or sit beside him to affirm in him the gift he had been to them. Each time, he offered them a blessing too, reminding them to keep on following the Lord and be strong in Him.

When we visited the doctor at the beginning of October, he said Norman's liver was much bigger than just ten days before. The cancer seemed to be progressing much faster than he'd anticipated. In light of that progression Norman asked how much time he may have left. Doctor Hoch said although one couldn't ever be sure, he thought perhaps two weeks.

On the way home, I asked Norman how he felt about that prediction. Norman said, "For me, it is great relief. I know it isn't that way for you, but for me, I am glad."

After I had time to catch my breath, I told Norman that I had tried to do all I could to have faith and give him courage to fight and to live well, but if the time had come that he couldn't keep living, I would walk that way with him and help him to die well.

We had spent many hours that summer and fall reading

the Psalms together, rejoicing in the honesty of the psalmist.

We echoed the psalmist's expressions of fear and despair, and also his absolute faith that God loved him and saw him in his times of trouble.

Just like the psalmist, we had confidence that God would pick us up out of the deepest pits of difficulty and anguish. We felt an incredible mixture of absolute faith that healing and continued life here on earth could still come, and absolute resignation of our desires to God's greater wisdom.

One evening, less than a week before the end, Norman asked who else was in the room. I told him we were alone. He replied with deep assurance, "Oh no, we're not alone, there is someone else here."

When I pursued it, he surmised there were angels present.

Two nights before he died, our daughter Loralyn and I were sitting with him. I read the 23rd Psalm to him. When I came to "Even when walking through the dark valley of death I will not be afraid, for you are close beside me, guarding, guiding all the way," (TLB) he squeezed my hand, so I read it over again.

He whispered, "I'm not afraid, I'm just waiting, waiting!"

Suddenly, he held my hand up to my chest and asked, "You are ready to let me go, aren't you?"

Although my heart cried, I replied, "Yes, my love, you can go whenever God calls you."

He held me close and told me, "You've been a good wife—the very best!"

The next evening, I went to bed with him for the last time. I held his hand and he squeezed it several times.

Early in the morning of October 14, I heard him enthusiastically say, "Yes, yes, yes!"

There was unqualified happiness and joy in his voice as

he repeated it several times. He was seeing something I could not. A little later he began with relief and gladness, to whisper "Home," with each breath.

I assured him, "Yes, Norman, you can go home."

I called our daughter and his sister to come, then I laid my head on the pillow beside his ear and sang "Lead me gently home, Father."

When I came to the last line, I repeated it several times— "Lead me gently, home, Lead me gently home." By that time his breaths were extremely shallow and far apart. We watched as the last few breaths came. Just as the sun rose above the horizon, the lines on his forehead disappeared, and he was at home and at peace.

What a precious moment! Time and eternity, at that instant, did not feel far apart. The room was full of the glory of God's presence. I felt a little like I had when I rocked the children to sleep, then laid them in the crib, continuing to sing until I was sure they were completely at rest. I could only cry, "Thank-you, Jesus, thank-you, Jesus!"

The Second Time Around

Ruth Smith Meyer

It seemed like a bit too much. Paul and I had been married only two weeks. The doctor sat behind his desk that mid-December day in 2005, stating the outcome of the biopsies—all twelve cancerous, ten of them aggressive in nature.

Six years before, I had heard a similar pronouncement when Norman, my first husband, was diagnosed with colon cancer.

Like an athlete, I had laid aside everything else for the task ahead. I had concentrated on the goal before me—to do everything to help my husband achieve all he could, then help him die well. I cared for him through sleepless nights and waning strength. Seven months later, I said goodbye to the dear one whose life I shared for thirty-nine years.

After six years of widowhood, a joyous miracle brought me Paul, another kind, loving man. Our hearts were filled with exuberance. At our age, we could possibly have twenty years of marriage—a real bonus neither of us expected. God definitely led us together. We were filled with blissful expectancy. But with the doctor's prediction, we wondered if we would now have only seven months. Figuratively, I reached for my running shoes.

Paul told me early in our relationship that he was scheduled to have knee replacements the following year. We had hoped we could then go on long walks, explore the wooded areas on his farm and travel to different places we both wanted to see. In February, he had his prostate removed, followed by a knee replacement in April. Before the end of the year, he had thirty-five radiation treatments and another knee replacement, followed by a severe infection from the radiation.

We joked that we were just taking care of all "the worse" of our wedding vows right away so we could get on with "the better." We still hoped for better days and some of those activities.

The next spring Paul experienced drop-foot. Over the next years he went through periods of extreme pain, back surgery, hour upon hour sitting in hospital and doctors' waiting rooms. The love God gave us for each other kept us content and strong through it all. But we were also constantly aware of how tenuous our time together was and how quickly our togetherness could come to an end. We did have some good times. We travelled to Alberta several times, once going all the way to Vancouver to visit his grandson. It was his first trip through the mountains. He was awed and felt our time together was almost like a honeymoon even though it was three years after our wedding.

In July of 2015, when Paul became unable to walk, he spent three months in hospital and rehab. He came home just before Thanksgiving, wheelchair bound, but exercising with his walker several times a day. The last of the options for treatment had failed, so we knew there wasn't much time left. We were delighted to mark our 10th anniversary in December. His son and family came from Alberta to spend Christmas with us. For the first time in many years, the whole family celebrated that holiday together. We took pictures and enjoyed our three great-grandsons.

January 6, Paul was again hospitalized. He seemed to be coming along well, then early on the morning of the 15th, a call came to say he had a gastro-intestinal bleed from which he wouldn't recover.

I called his daughters and my children and left for the hospital. Most of the grandchildren, too, were able to visit him in the next day and a half. We talked together and he joined in, even joking at times. One of the grandchildren asked: "What is the meaning of all the bracelets of various colours?"

There was a twinkle in his eyes, then he answered, "I don't know what they all mean, but the yellow one means 'Call before you dig.'"

Saturday afternoon we noticed swelling in his extremities. He seemed to be getting restless. When asked about this change, the nurse said, "It's because we're giving him intravenous and his kidneys have shut down."

"So why are you giving him intravenous?" I asked

"Well, it will help him last a little longer," the nurse replied.

His daughters and I looked at each other, and I voiced what I knew we were all thinking.

"We know where he's going and we don't want to make him more uncomfortable. Please don't start another bag."

"It won't be long, if I don't start it," she warned.

"That's okay," we reassured her.

One of the granddaughters began to sing "I can only imagine." Paul's face relaxed and we kept singing until his breathing ceased. Our time together on earth was over.

Now I needed my running shoes for a different race—that of learning to live alone again. There was, and continues to be, a reluctance to face such deep grief a second time. In the months following Paul's death, my uppermost emotional response was thankfulness for the ten years we were given to enjoy together.

When it came close to a year after Paul's death, that thankfulness began to feel a bit like a dam that was keeping my true grief from flowing freely. I anticipate having to do some work to process and deal with that. I have certainly found it true that no two grief journeys are the same. Grief for a husband with whom you finished growing with, parented with, struggled through marriage crises and found renewed love and commitment with, and welcomed grandchildren with, was life-jolting anguish.

The love between Paul and me also was precious and deep. We went through trials of our own. Our time together was unique. Because it was an unexpected bonus of love and a marriage of ten years, it is a distinctly dissimilar experience from the first journey of this kind. Perhaps being seventeen years older makes a difference too.

The lonely days and nights, the missing of companionship and physical touch are realities and a similar struggle as before. It is still too soon to tell the full story of my grief this time around, but it's already been a revelation of how diverse and distinctive grief can be.

At the Hospice, April 18th

Carolyn Wilker

I sit by Dad's bed at the hospice, and besides the sound of my pen moving across the paper, the only other sounds are the hum of the small refrigerator behind me and Dad's soft breathing. In and out, his lips moving in sync with the outward breath. The clock ticks as the second hand moves from one number to the next.

The sound of trucks and cars moving along the road are not as noticeable, since the hospice is tucked back on the property. If the outside door was open, we might hear the birds chirping. Regrettably, the screen is broken in the outer door and needs repair and so it's set aside for now until a volunteer can fix it. This place operates and functions by the help of many hands.

I look across the field and watch the sun glinting off the glass windshields as cars go down the hill, and I glance around the room at the spent blooms of the potted daffodils and tulips on a table near the hall door. There are still a few flowers, but I have pinched off the blooms that are sad and done. I think of this as such an appropriate place, away from the rush of the city, and in the country as Dad has been accustomed to all his life.

Mom has gone home and it's just Dad and me. He's doesn't yet know that I'm here, he's so tired. I wonder if he sleeps much at night or whether he lays awake wondering how long this dying will take. Is he afraid? Does he worry about pain? If he does, he hasn't spoken much about it. The palliative team monitors and makes sure that Dad is not in pain.

In the distance, I hear a train whistle, not so loud from

here, but I know there's a stop near the manufacturing plant on the next concession. Other than those sounds, I pay attention to the thoughts whirling around in my head. They can be loud at times, especially at night when I awake from sleep, but they are not foreign in the daytime either.

There are quiet times when Dad sleeps. And then I wonder how much time is left for our father, for any of us

really. We don't talk a lot about that, but we recognize it as part of our life, that at some time it will be over. Hard stuff to think about, but it's a reality. And it's often hard to put into words. Maybe Dad just doesn't want to talk about it.

I know life is short, relatively speaking, and time left to Dad is even shorter now. My heart may not be ready when the time comes, but my head knows and accepts that the place he approaches—that I hope we all see—will be much kinder and more beautiful than we can imagine.

Going to the hospice isn't an issue for me. It's like a magnet, something I need to do, to be there as often as I can. I've cut back on other commitments for the time being. Fewer work hours and suspended volunteer duties.

Leaving here is the harder thing. We don't want Dad to feel alone. Also, maybe because we never know if this is the last day for him, or for us to be together. If I think about it too long, the tears come and my throat feels like it's closing up. No, I cannot say I'm evading the inevitability of Dad's death. The truth is it's there every time I ring the doorbell to enter the hospice. It's with me all the way there, and all the way home. I think about it every day when I'm at home. It surrounds me, but I try my best to work through those whirling emotions.

It's a sense of belonging and closeness that calls me here so often. My father was available to us when we were children. He made time for play and built things for us, teaching us much. He was always there when we wanted to talk with him. It's a two-way street. Needing to be there, for Dad and for ourselves. I feel good about being here, even when it's hard, when the tears come.

As I spend more time at the hospice, I feel a restlessness and it's hard to sit. A stroll down the hallway, a short visit with the volunteers; it all helps. The volunteers are kind and thoughtful. They're here for the patient first, but they believe their mission is also to support the families of their patients.

My mind sweeps back to this vanilla-coloured room when the nurse comes in to give Dad a needle, but she gently tells him first what she is about to do. A temporary awakening, if only partial, from his sleep, he winces at the needle insertion. She checks the port where they give his meds and looks up to acknowledge my presence. The staff and volunteers make it a peaceful spot for one's last days.

Outside, a heavy truck lumbers up the hill. Probably loaded with heavy cargo—sand, soil or rocks perhaps.

There's more traffic on the road now, but it's still far enough away not to be a disturbance to Dad or me. At nearly 5:30 p.m. people may be making their way home after work.

Home is calling me too and Dad is still sleeping. I've been here if he needed something or even to see that one of his family members was beside him.

Is home calling Dad as well?

The Poem

Carolyn Wilker

We'd been raised in a Christian home knowing there's a new home awaiting us—another place beyond this earthly life where we go when we die. All is not over at the last breath. Still, death means a separation from the one we love. That's the hard part, because I loved my Dad.

I could no more keep quiet about Dad being in hospice than stop breathing. While driving back and forth to Woodstock, I realized that I needed to work through my feelings. I thought about the time I spent with him while other activities were on hold. It was very real, dealing with the further decline in his health, and so I wrote a blog post where it was least likely to upset anyone in my family, particularly my mother. Few family members had ever commented on my blog posts unless I shared the link with them in an email, but it could have helped others and it certainly helped me to write it out and process my thoughts.

I carried a notebook constantly when I was away from home so I could write out my feelings and observations. During those eleven weeks while Dad was in hospice, I felt I was on a precipice that at any moment could give way and send me hurtling into the depths of sadness and chaos. Dad was slowly losing his physical ability and seemed more uncomfortable. Other days he slept a lot. He couldn't get out of bed and walk anymore. We started to get a sense of his decline when he no longer wished to do something he had always enjoyed—doing jigsaw puzzles.

Hospice was a serene and beautiful place for his last weeks, a kind place to spend time with him.

My Mom, sisters and I brought pictures of family and

were there as often as possible. We brought some of his favourite foods too—applesauce, maple syrup, fresh fruit—and on one of the earlier visits, my sister brought in fish and chips for family members who were there, and Dad enjoyed some too. We had a feast right there in his room with him.

Mom had clipped a poem from the newspaper months before and had asked me to write a similar one with themes such as trees and birds. We'd use it for his funeral service. She was already planning ahead, knowing the day was coming. As sad and difficult as it was, we knew that day would come, and soon.

I found it difficult to write the kind of rhyming verse as the author whose poem she had given to me. I had to find my own way.

One night in March, during those hospice days, I started writing. The poem evolved as I wrote and revised.

My poem was intended for Dad, so I'd share it with him. We could read it at the service later, but I wanted him to hear it. He was asleep the day I arrived with the freshly printed paper in my hand. I handed the paper to Mom while we sat in the sunny area next to the kitchen, after she gave us our daily update. She looked up from reading the poem and said, "I like it. I have to reread it." And she smiled.

"Dad gets to hear it," I said. "After all it's for him."

When Mom went to check on Dad, I shared the piece with two hospice volunteers on duty.

One said, "I couldn't read it out loud without crying." She put the paper down and said, "A poem like this would be good for grief counselling." She remarked on the humour and said it would bring some lightness when it's most needed.

I was pleased. "Sure, you can use it. After I share it with Dad." And I handed it to her to make a copy, because I was still waiting to read it to my father.

Dad was not a big poetry reader, but he'd liked what I'd shared before, especially as it related to our life on the farm. He was awake and the bed had been wound up to a comfortable sitting position in his vanilla-coloured private room. The fleece blanket that my sister Joan had made lay across him to keep him warm. I sat in the chair beside him.

"How are you doing?"

He shrugged his shoulders just a bit, but it was clear he was glad to see me.

"Dad, I wrote something for you. Would you like to hear it?"

"Sure." And he sat quietly listening while I read.

Not Just a Dream

I awoke from a dream   you'd been there
letting me try on your shoes   so much bigger than my small feet
gathering me in your arms   calming my fears
teasing me back to smiles   by the time you set me down

Awakening from a dream   you'd been in the middle of it
pushing me on the swing
balancing me on the teeter totter
giving me piggy back rides
and whisker rubs before you shaved

I awoke from a dream   you'd handed me a ball and glove
taught me to throw and catch
getting me ready for the baseball games to come
and skating in winter between the corn stalks   then our very own rink
you gave me time

The dream faded   but you were there no mistake
teaching me to drive a tractor   pull a plough

stacking bales we were a team
loading that wagon with hay or straw
my sister driving up and down the raked rows

The dream vanished   but it was you there with us
picking cucumbers   your hands as green as ours
from gathering   sorting and bagging
then digging potatoes   we're as brown as the earth
by the time we were done

The dream   you'd been there beside me
in the passenger seat
teaching me to start and stop on a hill, watching as
I practise parked
between straw bales   knowing that neither the car
nor I would be hurt
pass or fail   you were there while I tried the test
and ready
if I needed a few more lessons

The dream curtain parted again   you smiled proud
as you walked me up the   aisle to meet my groom
—it didn't matter whether it was grass or carpet,
outdoors or in—
and gave your little girl one more hug

Unmistakable, your grin as I awoke from a dream
you'd been smiling at your newest grandchild who'd
someday
help you find the violets in the bush
watching for chattering squirrels and
make paths in the sandbox where we once played

You've been with us
graduation
confirmation

affirmation that you loved us

That wasn't a dream
and we loved you for it.

Dad lay back on his pillow and thought about it, then grinned that sideways grin he had. "I had a feeling the tester would take you to the same place," he said.

I knew which part he was talking about. The driving lessons, and me having troubles with the car rolling backwards as I stopped on a hill in Stratford, with his standard Chevy.

We recalled, there in his hospice room, the driving lessons he'd given among other things.

Dad asked me to put the poem on the bulletin board in his room. He'd never said as much before about what I'd written though he was at my first book launch to support my efforts. But for this personal piece, about him, he was clearly touched. That meant a lot to me.

Emotion swelled in me as I put the poem up on his white board. Dad had never said much about my work any other time, though he was never stingy with his love and he was always available to us at our school concerts, at other special events such as confirmation. His words had often been few.

He just gave us that warm smile as his blue eyes crinkled

in the corners; a smile like his Mom's.

Not long after when my nephew, Drew, came with his three young children, Dad pointed out the poem. "Drew, read that poem on the board."

Drew moved toward the board and read while his children played in the room. By now, there was more than a feeling of pride in my efforts. Tears stung at the edge of my eyes. This was praise that I'd not heard much of, ever.

We took a lot of memory journeys in those eleven weeks at hospice—a conversation on Skype with Mom and Dad's friends in a nursing home in Kapuskasing, the video my sister Kim had made with all our photos to celebrate Dad's 90th birthday in January of the same year, and more. All to help him pass time in as pleasant a way as possible. All the while, we knew this wouldn't go on forever, but we'd enjoy the time we had with him. He knew and was preparing himself for it too. Mom and Dad's pastor had stopped in a number of times as well.

We were preparing ourselves for the inevitable, even though it would be difficult when that day came. Every day we went to the hospice, we faced that knowing one day his spirit would soar again. And only God knows our last days and hours.

A Legacy

Glynis M Belec

As I pressed the sponge to clean the slightly faded yellow paint in my bathroom in preparation for a new coat, I suddenly remembered. Jim painted these walls. Going on seven years ago. He was so patient. So agile. He didn't even grumble when I switched from bright teal to soft yellow.

"No problem," he had said. "You have to like it. I don't mind changing it." So he did. With a smile on his face and a servant's attitude, he painstakingly covered the colour I had first chosen.

Jim was like that. Before his body was ravaged by Amyotrophic Lateral Sclerosis (ALS)[10] he led a busy life. Not only was he a loving husband, dad and grandpa, he also served faithfully as a council member in our town for over 21 years. He was highly respected and helped many people in his church and community, sitting on different committees and advocating for the rights and needs of others. He was a hard worker and always gave one hundred percent to whatever the task was—even painting my bathroom wall.

Jim's family and close friends knew he wasn't perfect and sometimes his busyness interfered with downtime, but there was never any question about the love he had for them.

"I miss my Dad," Karina, Jim's eldest daughter, said. "I miss his laugh and his cheerful voice on the phone when I called home."

Trish, Karina's younger sister, said, "I miss seeing the joy

---

[10] Also known as Lou Gehrig's Disease. A progressive neuromuscular disease in which nerve cells die and leave voluntary muscles paralyzed.

on Dad's face every time my family travelled from our home in Wisconsin back to small town Drayton, Ontario, to see him."

There are so many reasons a daughter misses her Daddy. Karina and Trish could make endless lists of what they miss the most, from golf lessons to financial advice to mission trip conversations to the lessons about casting a line in search of the perfect catch on a solitary lake. They would miss vacationing together. They will never forget that last special family holiday in a cozy cabin on a bright July day. Less than a week into their time together, their Dad had trouble swallowing and breathing. The family had been enjoying sharing sweet memories and treasured laughter. Jim was taken to hospital for the last time.

"It was so painful watching him suffer while he was alive," Karina said, "not knowing if he was at peace while struggling with the terrible symptoms of ALS."

Gut-wrenching images invaded her thoughts as she wondered how her father would die. "Would he suffer during the last moments? How was mom holding up?"

Trish had similar thoughts. It hurt to see their father lose his ability to speak and walk and eventually swallow. When he did succumb to the ravages of the disease, both girls were broken hearted, but they also confessed that it was not quite as hard as they had expected.

Karina said, "I found I was finally at peace because he was at peace. He was no longer suffering and he was set free!"

Her grief changed from frustration and anxiety to sadness. "I miss him incredibly, but I would rather him be with Jesus than suffering with us."

"God gets me through each day," Trish said. "I imagined it would be tougher after Dad's passing. But now I know God had been holding me even before I found out the news and

He continues to do so."

Jim left a legacy of love and hope and faith to his family. It doesn't make grieving any easier. It does, however, lessen the sting and offer comfort.

"It's essential for us to grieve," Karina said. As a health care professional, she knows how bottling up grief can be unhealthy.

"Grief becomes negative when we deal with it negatively—eating poorly, isolating ourselves, getting angry quickly, hurting ourselves."

Karina admits that she tried her best to be positive after her father's death. "I think my grief was mostly positive. I understood why I was feeling the way I did. I allowed myself to experience many emotions."

Both girls turned their sadness into gratitude—thankful they had someone so special in their life to grieve over. "I found in those deep moments of sadness I was able to feel God's embrace," Karina said.

Trish admits she came to grips with her grief weeks after her father died. She was watching her young daughter peel a Band-Aid from her knee.

"She had fallen off her bike and had hit the pavement earlier. A Band-aid covered her wound and had taken away a little of her pain. As time passed the wound began to heal. It was then she decided to slowly pull off the Band-Aid."

Trish saw this as an analogy to her grief. Like the wound, losing her Dad to ALS had been painful. The deep sadness and crippling grief she first felt was the bandage covering that gaping wound that cut deeply. The pain was intense and she didn't think she would ever heal. In time, the Lord slowly removed the Band-aid. Complete healing wouldn't happen overnight.

Jim taught his family and friends much, in life and in

death. When you receive a diagnosis for which there is no cure, you discover how fleeting life is. After Jim's death, the family discovered that grief can be a good way to reconnect with a loved one. They watched him trust God when his world was caving in. He taught them that faith in a Divine plan is better than giving up and having no hope.

One of the biggest lessons they learned was that holding tightly to things in this world is fruitless. Holding on to God is what matters. Death does not have the final victory. Christ does. The whole family looks forward to a heavenly reunion one day and somehow, that lessens the sting of death and brings them a kind of peace that defies understanding.

As I look at the pale-yellow walls in my bathroom, I change my mind for now. I don't think it needs another coat of paint after all. I have more important things to attend to—like calling my children or hugging my husband or telling my own dad how much I love him.

Part 3
UNEXPECTED GRIEF

When Babies Die

Glynis M Belec

Aglowing young mother presses close to her husband in the delivery room. Expectant arms wait to hold their new baby, Wendy. They have come to the delivery room prepared with a name, but they have not come prepared for what was about to follow.

"Is something wrong?" Bobbi asked.[11]

A moment that was supposed to be filled with joy and excitement was soon turned into a time of uncertainty and confusion as Bobbi and Rick's precious newborn daughter was whisked away to the Neonatal Intensive Care Unit.

Wendy survived for thirty-seven hours. Her undeveloped lungs couldn't sustain her tiny breaths. Wendy slipped into a forever sleep as Bobbi and Rick slipped into each other's arms—in agonizing grief.

It hasn't been easy. Rick and Bobbi have travelled down the perilous road of grief with all its twists and turns. They've experienced the usual gamut of emotions one might expect over the years, but the one thing that Bobbi said, that made it the most difficult, was the unexpected manifestation of these emotions.

"I'd be doing fine," Bobbi said, "and suddenly grief would

---

[11] Junior, Bobbi; When the Bough Breaks ©2016

ambush me without warning."

Early on, triggers were different on any given day—an advertisement for baby clothes; hearing her two-year-old daughter laugh; passing by the doorway of what was to have been Wendy's bedroom.

"Sometimes none of these were an issue. But then, POW, gut-wrenching sobs would burst from my chest, as uncontrollable as a sneeze."

It didn't matter where Bobbi was, or how much she wanted to maintain control.

"These ambush events were in charge," Bobbi said. "I learned to pull over to the side of the road, if I was driving when one of them struck."

Sometimes her two-year-old daughter wondered what was wrong with Mommy when that happened.

"I made a point of telling Andrea that Mommy can cry, but she could still be happy."

It was important to Bobbi to let her little girl know that. just because Mommy was upset, she didn't have to be.

Life is supposed to be a story replete with a clear beginning, a well-defined middle and a satisfying conclusion. When a baby dies, the story is interrupted and becomes fragmented, incomplete and disjointed.

Parents shouldn't have to bury their children. Bobbi and Rick knew that but they also knew God was in control. Deep sadness enveloped this young couple, but they stayed away from anger.

"My personality is such that I get angry over very little," Bobbi said. "If God chose to take this baby, that was His right."

Bobbi found comfort in many things, including knowing that she'd had a good, happy, healthy pregnancy—up until her labour and delivery.

For a while she was confused, wondering if perhaps she had done something wrong that might have caused Wendy's medical condition. She and Rick were assured by the medical community that the Congenital Diaphragmatic Hernia (CDH)[12] that caused Wendy's death occurred during the early stage of pregnancy as the diaphragm was being formed and certainly did not happen because of things they had done wrong.

Grieving for a baby involves something different than grieving for someone who has had many years on this earth. Bobbi strongly felt this was true. She acknowledged there is a physical and spiritual connection between a mother and a baby that doesn't exist in the same way as a love relationship joins others.

Her theory was confirmed through an experience she had when her first daughter, Andrea, was a newborn. The nurse had come to draw some of Bobbi's blood for routine testing. She told her to watch her daughter when the needle went it.

"I watched, and Andrea's little body jerked as though she'd been pricked."

The nurse told Bobbi this was common, and it only happened once—where the mother feels a sudden pain and then baby does, too, at the same time. It's that connection that seemed to intensify the grief. Even though the external love was brief, the internal connection went deeper.

Bobbi describes her grief as a weight—something draped over her, like a chain-mail shroud. As much as she wanted to remove it, even for a brief time, to gain some respite from the burden, it somehow didn't seem possible. As the years

---

[12] A birth defect that develops as a fetus is forming in the mother's uterus. A congenital diaphragmatic hernia (CDH) occurs when the diaphragm does not form properly.

progressed, however, Bobbi found she built the emotional strength to carry the weight, like a jogger who wears weights on her ankles and eventually gets used to carrying around the extra weight.

"That's what happens with grief, I think," Bobbi said.

"We don't 'get over it'. Rather, it becomes part of us. We develop a new normal."

Rick and Bobbi were members of a church, and they were grateful for the way the ladies surrounded them with support. Because there were several who stepped in to help, none had to bear the full weight of their sorrow. They could share it, but then go on with their lives and let someone else step in. Support by a group was good for Bobbi, because she didn't like feeling she was taking advantage of someone's kindness. She had the support she needed, but without the guilt of being a burden.

As Bobbi looked back over the years, she realized that telling her story over and over again shifted the memory of Wendy's life and death from extraordinary to ordinary. She's since learned that this is an aspect of trauma counselling—to talk about what happened, and process it a bit more each time.

Bobbi saw Wendy as having a perfect soul. She didn't have to live a lifetime to gain the lessons needed before going back to her Father in heaven. Bobbi felt privileged to be Wendy's mother.

"Was that a fanciful way to view it?" Bobbi wonders. "Perhaps." But she says that approach has helped her through some of her saddest times.

As Bobbi dealt with deep sadness, she appreciated when people offered her a simple invitation to talk. 'Tell me about today' was a good way to get her to open up. Bobbi said it's important to let people know you are comfortable around them, even though you are grieving.

"They don't have to dial it down when you're around."

When people would preface their words with 'at least' Bobbi shuddered a little. When you have lost a baby, there is no comfort in knowing that 'at least she's back in the arms of Jesus' or 'at least you have another child at home' or 'at least she's not suffering.'

"Don't try to be profound, wise or helpful," Bobbi suggests. "Just ask questions, occasionally, and listen."

Sometimes we tell those who are dealing with the death of a baby that they're inspiring. Or they have a strong faith. Bobbi suggested those are not helpful comments.

"Don't say 'I don't know how you're managing' or 'I could never do this.'"

Bobbi said these kinds of remarks suggested that the person grieving is responsible for making others feel okay about the death of a child.

"Better to say nothing at all."

Both Rick and Bobbi know that death is part of life.

"By loving others," Bobbi said, "we are saying we're willing to accept the grief that might come as a result. Grief is evidence of a great depth of emotion, and that's never a bad thing."

Rick and Bobbi have had many reasons to find joy. Bobbi got pregnant within a year of Wendy's death, so a lot of their energies were poured into their growing family. But they always remembered their little Wendy. They made sure their children knew her as their 'sister in heaven', too.

Bobbi believes that nothing in this world happens without God's hand upon it.

"I don't have to know and understand and control what goes on. I just need to do the best I can."

When she thinks like that, she says it lets her off the hook for feeling responsible for what she can't control. That gives her comfort.

Something else that gives her comfort is accepting that grief doesn't go away. But Bobbi's okay with that. Because the way she sees it, grief is the evidence of love and of richness of life.

Wendy's life was short but overflowing with the fullness and love of family. [13]

---

[13] Bobbi Junior has written a book about her experience as a grieving mother; When the Bough Breaks ©2016, Angel Hope Publishing; ISBN 9781988155036.

One Day at a Time

Glynis M Belec

The one year anniversary of my niece's death brought with it tribute after tribute on social media. A beautiful young mother, thirty-six years old, dead from a heart attack. She left behind a loving husband, a teenage daughter, a special needs son, parents who had already lost one daughter in a car accident. Two brothers and so many other family members and countless friends and coworkers also mourned her death.

Unexpected death wrenches the heart and tears at the soul. There is no preparation, no warning, and no apparent reason. Death of a loved one is sad whenever it happens, but when it tears, unannounced, into the fabric of family, it is so difficult to make sense of the loss. Questions abound and anger permeates the grief. Tears flow to the point of exhaustion.

A year had passed since April's death. But the pain still rippled through our tightly knit family like it was yesterday. As I read through the tributes, I cried soft tears reliving the moments when family and close friends gathered at Roy and April's home after hearing the devastating news.

April was a hard-working young mom with a beautiful smile and a heart for family. She wasn't without stress—but to the point of a heart attack? No one was more shocked than Roy, her husband of 13 years.

"I had no clue," Roy said over and over to those who asked if April had heart problems. Even April's parents had no idea. And Roy was quick to say the doctor was just as shocked. There was no indication that April's life would be snapped away so suddenly by cardiac arrest.

April's brother, Nathan, had rushed to the hospital the minute Roy had called him. After it was confirmed that April had not made it, Roy and Nathan embraced for what seemed an eternity. A loving wife. A beautiful sister. Gone.

Nathan managed to get to a telephone. He knew he needed to call his mother, Jeannette. It was the worst call he ever had to make.

"I think I went into shock because I know I froze for a few minutes," Jeannette said after Nathan told her what happened. She eventually managed to call her other son, Jeremy, before she headed to the hospital where Roy and Nathan sat weeping in disbelief.

Later, Roy was the one who woke April's father, Paul, to tell him the heart-wrenching news.

"I thought he [Paul] was going to have a heart attack himself."

When Roy talks even now, about that tortuous moment when he had to utter those words, "April is dead," to his father-in-law, the tears flow. The sting is still there.

A grieving husband. Lost. Confused. Yet he turned to his weeping father-in-law and assured him, "We'll get through this together."

My heart broke for Jeannette and Paul when I saw them after we heard the news. They could barely figure out what to do. The shock heaving through the entire family was unbearable at times. Jeannette and Paul had already lost a daughter in a tragic car accident many years prior. It was a sickening blow to realize that another child, another precious daughter, was gone. Forever.

"I felt my heart break in two," Jeannette said, between tears. "But I knew I had to think of the kids first."

Roy and April's two children, Corryn, 12, and Zander, 10, were their world. The thought of telling them their mother had died was ripping Roy's heart from his chest.

Corryn had a good relationship with her mother. She was growing up and blossoming into a lovely young woman. Zander was a beautiful boy who had had mobility issues and learning challenges from birth.

Both April and Roy had their hands full, but they went about their days with joy and a great attitude. Suddenly it had all blown apart.

"I dreaded hearing the bum-scooting down the hallway," Roy said, referring to the way Zander moved around without his wheelchair or other mobility devices.

"I told them God called Mom to her heavenly home," Roy said, weeping at the recollection. Then Zander said something that made him sit up and wonder.

"I don't know why, Dad, but I am happy." Zander was convinced his mother was in the right place and was at complete peace. A special needs child making such a pronouncement? "Sometimes I wonder if they know more than we give them credit for," Roy said, after hearing his son's tender words.

Corryn was broken-hearted and wept quietly, but it seemed she was relieved her brother handled the news well. Family gathered. Corryn had lots of support from close family members and friends so she was rarely alone and knew she could lean on those she loved at any time of the day or night.

When I spoke to Jeannette recently, I asked how she was coping. She smiled that motherly smile and said, "One day at a time."

She's living out her pledge to think of the kids first. And she does that by being a fabulous Mémére [grandmother] to Corryn and Zander and her other grandchildren.

Roy says he copes by thinking about people who are in worse situations. I feel humbled hearing his compassionate response. How much worse can a situation be, I wonder?

"In the 13 years we were married, I think we shared more love than some do in 50 years," Roy said. "I find it helps when I focus more on the memories of April than on the loss."

That was pretty good advice coming from a young man who hadn't dealt much with death. He was the first to admit he didn't know how to handle April's death, but he sure does know where to put his focus.

"I was lucky to know her. I was lucky to have been loved by her, and because of that great love, I feel like my life with April was fulfilled, albeit too short."

Roy admits he will never stop grieving for April. He also knows he has a long road ahead of him filled with appointments, challenges, terrific teenagers and so much more. His grief is offset knowing that April would be proud of him. He was secure in their love. He knows she loved him for who he was. All he can do is his best.

Every time I talk to him, I am inspired by his best and his smile and the obvious love he has for his children. When I look at their family pictures, I can't help but feel a heavy sadness envelop me. Then I think of his joy-filled attitude with a heavy focus on moving forward despite the crushing pain that threatens a scarred heart.

Jeannette said to me recently, "Everyone feels differently about death. But the best way to deal with grief is to talk about the person who has died. Even if it makes the loved one cry."

Here we are a year later, still seeing the outpouring of love and the way that family and friends continue to rally together, sharing the excruciating pain of missing a mother, a wife, a daughter, a sister, an aunt, a niece, a cousin, a friend.

Roy purchased sealed necklaces, containing April's ashes,

for the immediate family to wear close to their hearts. It was Corryn's idea. She wanted to find a way to keep her mother near.

Tears fall sometimes when we remember April's beautiful twinkling eyes and her love of family. We will treasure the memories. We will talk about her when it's appropriate. We will check in with one another, because that's what families do. Laughter happens because love prevails. April would like that.

Life After Death

Glynis M Belec

"Oh God! I'll be right there."

My husband's voice still echoes in my mind. Like a trapped wolf howling for rescue, his voice took on another sound—a moan; a groan of agony; something that I hadn't heard before.

"It's Wayne. He's dead. Linda and Mom found him. He hanged himself."

I wanted to vomit. My eight-month pregnant body gave a dry heave and I didn't know what to do. Gilles did. He hugged me quickly and said he didn't know when he would be back. Then he jumped in his truck and headed for the city.

Gilles' six sisters and his one and only brother had not had it easy over the years. Their mother had almost singlehandedly raised her eight children. Her husband had fallen prey to the bottle years before, so their early life had been anything but stable. But she was a strong woman and had done her best to raise her children on limited income, never knowing if it was 'time to move' again.

But when Gilles' mother and younger sister, Linda, found Wayne, her strength was ripped away and she could hardly breathe. Her children were her Achilles' heel. Wayne's death was a blow that would affect the entire family forever.

Gilles and his older sister, Sue, took the reins and made the arrangements with the funeral home and did whatever else they had to do. The police were involved because by law, they were required to rule out anything suspicious. It didn't take long. The note and taped recording that Wayne left served as an affirmation that he had made the heartrending decision to end his own life.

Much of what happened is a blur. Everything seemed helter-skelter and because Gilles had a large extended family —many of whom I'd never met in the three years we were married—all I remember is a constant stream of people. Crying, shocked, stunned family and friends.

Gilles was so busy. He and Sue dealt with most of the funeral arrangements and formalities required after a family member dies. He felt it was his duty to step up and be strong for his six sisters and his heart-broken mother.

At times I was concerned because Gilles never shed a tear. He was stoic and steadfast in his duties. He greeted and soothed the sad. He tried to answer the myriad of questions. Why? What happened? Did anyone know?

Gilles was already dealing with his own questions.

"I was with Wayne the day before he died. Did I miss something? Why didn't I see signs so I could have got Wayne some help? Or, at least, intervened."

Sue felt the same. Wayne usually called her every day. They had a good relationship and many shared friends so Sue had similar questions.

"For days after the funeral," Sue said, "I reflected on his life. I loved him dearly. He was a good brother." Like the rest of the family, Sue cried a lot and thought about how she would miss his phone calls. Then she got to the point in her grief where she felt a tiny sense of relief for her deceased brother, because he was no longer suffering with mental anguish.

After the funeral and after everyone went home, the girls, Gilles, and his mom were left to pick up the pieces and try to make sense of what had happened.

Finally, three days after the funeral, Gilles cried. We were lying in bed talking about the past few days, going over what had happened and how things had changed.

Gilles was talkative and seemed to need to vent. It was good. He hadn't had a chance to share his own feelings, because he had been too busy looking after everyone else. But then the floodgates opened. He suddenly fell into my arms and began to weep. Inconsolably. I had never seen him so overcome with deep sadness and heartache. My heart hurt for my young husband. But I was glad he finally cried. And was honoured he did so in my arms.

The days passed. It was still hard to grasp what had happened. There I was, great with child, soon to give birth and the family was still reeling from Wayne's sudden death. I didn't have a relationship with God, although I often felt a great need to pray. But I was busy dealing with my own guilt. Mine was more focused on the sadness I might bring by giving birth. Sadness because my baby's life might heighten the grief of Wayne's recent death. I imagined Gilles' family would not accept my joy and happiness.

One day the doorbell rang. Friends of ours had told their pastor about what had happened. He was a kind man filled with love and compassion. At first we were a little hesitant to share details of our family and Wayne's death, but before we knew it, we had coffee on the table and we had poured out our entire story, and then some, to this quiet man who seemed to be listening with his soul.

There was no pressure, but he invited us to visit his church and to spend time talking to God and to other people who might know a bit of our pain. He left us Good News Bibles and suggested we start reading the Gospels. He prayed with us before he left. We were grateful.

Not too long after that, Gilles came home with a few items that his mother had given to him. It included a photo of Wayne and a Bible. When we opened the Bible, the little inscription on the inside read, 'My name is Wayne Joseph, and this very day I have given my life to Jesus.' Somehow that little inscription gave us a sense of peace.

Three weeks later our son was born. And there was great celebrating. Not sure if it was God softening my heart, but suddenly all the guilt I had been feeling was washed away. I started to understand that I was not the one who controlled life or death. Our baby boy was a gift, and we were excited to honour his uncle who he would never meet, by giving him his name—Trevor Wayne Gilles.

Gilles says he often thinks of his brother.

"Every time I hear of someone who has died by suicide, it comes rushing back. When I hear a song on the radio, or a phrase that he might have said, I think of Wayne."

We all miss Wayne. But we've learned over the years that by delving into those Gospels and digging more into the Word, God makes good out of tragedy and sadness. Gilles and I have learned that first-hand in many ways over the years.

We would give anything to have Wayne back, but that's not reality. The reality is that because of the heartbreak that happened so many years ago, we were started on our faith journey. We discovered after the birth of our son, and after the moment that we both accepted Jesus as our Saviour, there is life after death.

When I Stop Crying

Glynis M Belec

"Oh, God. Please, no! Not Bailey."

When I saw the headlines in the newspaper, I could hardly breathe. Sweet Bailey. Our waitress friend who we saw almost every Friday evening when we went on our date. Murdered. Her identity confirmed.

Her smile had captured our hearts when we met her over ten years ago. We had popped into the restaurant for one of our Friday date nights. Bailey was our server and when she asked me if I wanted the low-calorie dressing on my salad, I facetiously asked, "Do you think I need it? Are you saying I should pick the low-calorie option? What are you really saying?"

Poor Bailey. She tried so hard to back track and make amends for something she really did not say. But from that moment on, we became friends. Instantly. We laughed and she went to get my salad with the low-calorie dressing.

My husband and I made that restaurant a regular destination for a meal out and we always tried to sit in Bailey's section. But if we couldn't, that sweet blonde-haired dreamy-eyed sweetheart would make a point of finding a moment or two to come and chat and give us a hug. Once she paid for our meal with her own money. Another time when she found out that it was our anniversary, she made us a special dessert—no charge. She paid with her tips again—much to our protest, but she was determined.

A couple of times, Bailey had met us for dinner and we soon found out about some of her dreams, her adventures, and her free spirit. Not sure why she seemed to care so much about us. After all, we were old enough to be her parents, but she was genuine and spoke respectfully and encouragingly every time we met. She was the one who showed me how to text. Bailey had taken my old flip phone at the time and patiently walked me through the process. We had some good laughs as we did that.

I particularly remember one time after I had been going through chemotherapy, Gilles and I hadn't been to the restaurant for a while. But when Bailey saw me, bald as a baby, she came running up to me and hugged me and cried her eyes out. We all did. I felt like I was holding my own child as she kept reassuring me that things would be okay.

That summer evening when my hubby and I attended a funeral visitation that should not have been, we felt as if a little bit of our world had caved in. A young girl—28 beautiful years old—was being laid to rest. People came by the hundreds to share a brief moment with her family and to express their condolences for this great loss. The emotions were varied— anger, confusion, devastation. And so many questions.

God did not have Bailey here for a long time, but we discovered that evening at the funeral home, that she not only impacted us, but so many others were touched by her life, too. It was mind boggling.

It both warmed and broke my heart to see all the young people come in droves to share and show respect for their lost friend.

"To our special angel..." I wrote on the huge matted photograph of Miss Bailey. I couldn't help but cry as I watched the photographs circulate on the big screen TV while we waited in line to speak to the grieving family.

"That should be playing at her wedding, not at her funeral," I leaned over and whispered to my sad hubby." He squeezed my hand.

We'd never met Bailey's family before, but she had spoken so lovingly of them. And they were all so strong and gracious. I don't know how they did it.

As I shed tears all the way home from the visitation, I told God that I would gladly (well maybe not gladly, but surely) trade my life to get Bailey's back. But life doesn't work that way. God calls who He calls...I don't understand it right now, but I am convinced that one day, when I do cross into the Great Beyond, I will have all my questions answered and I will know.

As more news about Bailey's murder surfaced, and the trial for the person accused of her murder progressed, I clipped story after story from the newspaper. I collected them and put them in a little silver box. I don't know why I did that; perhaps it was my way of not forgetting my sweet Bailey. Perhaps this was a way for me to keep her memory close.

Life is fleeting. Sometimes it doesn't make sense. But one thing that does make sense is the lesson I learned from Bailey—love is what really matters, so I had better do my best to pass it on.

We haven't returned to the restaurant where Bailey worked since we learned of her death. One day we will, when the wound heals a little more. When I stop crying. When God tells me it's time.

It will be a Friday evening. We will walk in and place our order. I will ask for the low-calorie dressing, and we will smile.

Release the Pain—
Enjoy the Memories

Donna Mann

April 28, 1972. Although many years ago, this memory is as vivid as yesterday. The sun warmed the crisp April air. A hint of spring scented the air. Even as the visible signs of this season promised new life, my world froze, stopped and died.

Debbie, our adorable adopted two-year-old, once so energetic and full of life, curious about everything, drowned in the swimming pool.

The doctor, local police and our minister helped in their own way. People came and went—family, friends and neighbours. They brought sandwiches, squares and cookies on trays and in cardboard boxes, and their love.

Over time, some folks continued to ask why and attempted to give answers. Too often the rationale became religious. People attempted to define God's purpose in Debbie's death. Folks became authorities on God. Overused worn-out one-liners became rampant. The sincere became biblical scholars. Some infused my thinking with fire and brimstone, predestination, reincarnation and the ever-popular will of God. Confusion reigned.

Then there were those people who comforted without trying to fix, rescue or release me. I soaked this up like a sponge. People called on the phone to ask about the family—we responded with gratitude. They sent us cards with practical no-nonsense notes—we walked to the mailbox with expectation. Neighbours brought casseroles and tucked in little notes like, "Enjoy. We're thinking about you." Helpful words were life-giving. I held onto them and repeated them to myself and my family.

Eventually I concluded that God must have willed Debbie's death, I put the words "Not my Will but Thine" on her tombstone and walked away.

We moved from the property which had been our first home for twelve years. We built a new house and filled it with our energies. It compensated for thinking about loss but didn't give the peace for which I searched. With our children in school, I had too much time to myself. They played hockey in the winter and baseball in the summer, with music lessons all year long. Doug coached hockey, so the car and family were busy.

Overjoyed to find that I was pregnant, even though my doctor had said 'no more, Donna,' I was soon grief stricken with another miscarriage—one year to the day of Debbie's death.

After some time, I responded to the church women's invitations to bring egg-on-brown to luncheons, or come to play piano for the Sunday school classes. This gave me confidence, and I returned to serve in the church community.

This was a caring pool of believers; I leaned on them. I found new strength in my faith. I still felt stuck in my grief. I knew if I continued on this path, I would fade as an individual, a mother and a wife. Tending to the family's needs in their grief was difficult, but often easier than listening to myself.

Through the years I had met dedicated social workers. My mission-heart responded. I began studying through correspondence to major in sociology with a minor in social work. This gave me opportunities to write essays about life's issues and family development—both of which helped me to understand myself and family.

I continued to study through Supervised Pastoral

Education for laity and clergy in 1976. This introduced me to the realization that I had not dealt with my grief. Time had not healed. The grief waited for me. I realized that mourning and talking about loss differed greatly from working through the process of grief.

I reflected over the past and could see where I'd been seeking help. However, without an informed resource to hold me accountable, I moved in circles—praying, reading, listening, acknowledging bits and pieces here and there, but not gaining recovery. I heard statistics of family breakdowns after the death of a child, and I didn't want that to happen to our family. I registered in "Introduction to Grief 101" in 1977. Through journaling, regular attendance and raw honesty, I worked the grief process with intention.

As I talked about grief through the 80s, people asked for resources and I photocopied the journal from "Grief 101" many times and mailed it out. (This was prior to email). After revision, it became the book Winter Grief (2003).

Serving in my church community, seeking out groups and subjects, became definite steps to recovery. In spite of my desire for isolation, an inner strength won over. Regardless of my insecurities, I gained confidence.

I discovered how to recall memories and emotions by naming them so I could get through them, to release them. I learned helpful new phrases and words and incorporated them into my vocabulary. I thought in positive terms, including the beauty of life.

I could now remember Debbie without guilt, judgment or anger. I could remember her with gratitude. I didn't have to rationalize, give reason or excuse.

I didn't have to speak for God—only accept God's grace and mercy to empower me to care for myself and be the best mother and wife I could be for my family.

I rediscovered a loving God, of whom grief had only allowed glimpses. God had been there all the time waiting to comfort and console, to support and love us. I reclaimed the same God who nurtured me prior to the tragedy, and to whom I returned. God waited for me to accept grace and strength. I had those words removed from the tombstone.

The grief process interrupted my life, slowed down my plans and goals, demanded my attention and drained my energies. It insisted on being front and centre in my life appealing for attention, even when I denied it. I learned valuable lessons as I grieved. The more I understood the process into which I entered, the freer I became. It was a gift once I rested in it. Like a revolving light on a lighthouse, it gave me insight when helping myself and others.

The discoveries revealed in the grief process brought me full circle to the peace I'd experienced before Debbie's death.

Long ago, I reached my goal: to remember her with joy, gratitude and thanksgiving. I had allowed the pain to coat, smother and stifle memories. I walked through that pain in an accountable process. Only then could I capture previous memories and celebrate them.

I lost a few years of relating to Debbie because I veiled the grief process. Knowing this gives me a passion to compensate for that lost time by writing about grief and walking with others caught in sorrow or stuck in grief. No, I didn't lose Debbie. That would be unbearable. Most precious in this process is to gain the ability to remember and talk about the little girl who continues to live—in my heart, in my memory and in precious pictures. Yes, we have five children (one deceased).

Skipped Heart Beats

Alan Anderson

I thought of you tonight.
Do you sleep in heaven?
Does anyone tuck you in bed at night?
Do you dream sweet dreams?

Do you giggle and laugh?
Are you amazed at the life you have?
Do you marvel at your life in heaven?
A place where you are loved and safe.

If only I could see you for just a minute.
If only I knew that you are never alone.
If only we could walk hand in hand.
If only I could kiss and hug you ever so tight,
I would never let you go.

My wife and I love our six grandchildren. Their giggles, laughter and love help strengthen the beats of our hearts. Their personalities are vastly different from child to child. Each one is unique and loved beyond measure. We enjoy being with them at family gatherings where they all play together.

We are also grandparents to five children in heaven. They are our little ones who never made it to birth. Our family looked forward to the births of these children. Their parents especially anticipated a growing family, but like a vapour, their little lives vanished. Hearts were broken.

I have never read nor heard another grandfather express his grief related to pregnancy loss. I have no model of grief to follow.

I think of my grandbabies in heaven and imagine what life would be like with them. Would they resemble their parents? Or have any of my traits or my wife's? Might they have my quirky humour? Would we sing Beatles' songs for fun? Perhaps we would go to Disneyland as a family and have our photographs taken with Mickey Mouse and Goofy. I love Goofy. Maybe they'd like him too.

I'd want my grandbabies in heaven to know I'll take care of their mommies and daddies and that I'll play and have fun with their brothers and sisters.

For now, I'll be content with my dreams and imagination of them. I will continue to write about them from time to time. This helps me feel closer to them.

My experience as a grandfather, in relation to pregnancy loss, means an experience with profound sadness that lingers like a ghost unwilling to rest. Each time I've been told of yet another baby who died, I think of the first one. On the morning of Saturday, June 28, 2008, my family and I were enjoying the annual Scottish Highland Games. The day of the Games is always a day of fun when we gather with those of our Scottish heritage. In the midst of all the enjoyment and crowds of people, my daughter informed my wife and me that she had "miscarried" her baby. I have always disliked the term 'miscarriage.'

It was one of those times I'll never forget. My daughter was standing in front of me telling me that her baby had died. I saw on her face the sadness showing itself by her tears.

Part of me died too. I realized that dads couldn't fix some things, even when they wanted to. This didn't hurt my pride, but it crushed my heart. I experienced similar feelings when my daughter-in-law told me as well. I spent time with her, listening to the cries of a young woman who wanted to be a mom again.

I kept much of my sadness to myself. As the expert of my own grief, I knew this was emotionally unhealthy. I had to express my grief somehow, and so I turned to writing.

My grief journey included a need to write a story in memory of my little ones. I could not knit a baby blanket or sweater, or buy baby's first pair of shoes. I could, however, write a story of love and remembrance. I promised these babies they would not be forgotten.

The story told of my thoughts of the babies being in heaven. I guess I was trying to make sense out of these multiple losses. I found comfort in my faith that they were with God.

The news of each baby who died stunned me. At the time of writing the story, there were three babies to remember. My daughter and son-in-law had lost two and one daughter-in-law had lost one. After writing that story, there would be two more babies who never made it to birth. The parents never named the babies, yet they will always be remembered.

My daughter is one of my teachers in life. Giving birth to children has not been easy for her. She has experienced complications every time and has endured multiple pregnancy losses. She is also a survivor and has the personal resolve to see the gift that life is. She summed up whether to name the babies in the following way when she told me,

"May sound weird, but I like to think God gave them the perfect names. When I eventually get to heaven, I will know their names." I have continued to honour her statement here.

When my son and daughter-in-law's baby died, it was a lonely time for them. Perhaps my daughter-in-law especially felt alone. She certainly didn't feel supported by her doctor and this increased her feeling of being alone. She was not aware of any support groups for pregnancy loss nearby or someone who might understand how she felt. Somewhere along the line I listened to her. There were no words I could say that would make things better. I listened and that seemed to be all she needed. We have a close bond and she knows she can trust me.

I could not feel the pain of the parents who experienced the death of a child. I did, however, feel pain after hearing such devastating news. I cried each time it happened. In processing this, I realized there was nothing I could have done to save the baby. There was also nothing I could do to protect my children from this tragedy.

The first baby's death silenced me and I didn't know how to respond. It felt as if I were in a cold wilderness not knowing where to turn. This wilderness blocked me in with big thick trees that would not bend, and I couldn't find a path to move forward. The trees blotted out the sun. The wind that blew through the trees chilled me. It was as if I was frozen in time. Time itself did not matter. The wilderness, the trees, the cold wind, the standing of time, all helped me to withdraw for a while. I needed to be still. A baby had died. I couldn't grasp what that meant.

When I was told of the first baby, my heart skipped a beat. Since then my heart has skipped five beats. I will never have those beats back again. There were no worldwide announcements of their passing. Life continued as usual, as much as possible under the circumstances. I, however, loved them. In my mind, I held each baby in my arms and placed them in my heart. They are safe there.

With each baby who said goodbye before saying hello, it felt like the death of a mystery. How do I grieve a mystery? It was the loss of a person I never met, yet loved. Someone I grieve for and a life I mourn. I used words to express my feelings. My heart felt the loss of those grandbabies I never met.

When my grandchildren died, it was as though God dimmed the light of the stars and sun. It was a dark time. Each loss was like a sudden death to me. I asked myself, how would I process these deaths?

My mind assailed me. The world did not make sense. Children are supposed to be born and fussed over. The death of children doesn't seem proper to me. My reality, of course, dictated otherwise. My protestation seemed to fall on deaf ears.

The stories I love to write are those inspired by real people. As I contemplate the impact of pregnancy loss on my life, I realize I miss the five babies who went to heaven. Their stories were brief—their lives were here then suddenly gone. They left me with hope. Hope, to me, rests in a belief that there is a life beyond this one. A hope in a life that will not vanish. It is a hope born in the One who loves children. Jesus said, *Let the little children come to me, and do not hinder them, for the kingdom of heaven belongs to such as these.*[14]

---

[14] Matthew 19:14 NIV

Offstage

Carolyn Wilker

Enter stage left, exit stage right
or is it enter stage right, exit stage left?
Only it was all wrong
you exited too soon

Your role ended
before our performance was done
we were powerless to stop it

Unaware of the gravity
the rise in suspense
a trap door opens in the theatre floor
takes the actor out of the scene

The lines you were to say next
never spoken
—an outcome we feared in Act IV
dropping
the final curtain

Not the tolling[15]

Carolyn Wilker

"not the tolling of bells but the silence after"[16]

Not the tolling of bells
or the parade of people
come to see you

acknowledging your pain
that some understand
and others simply want to comfort

Not the tolling of church bells you'd expect
or the filled pews   but the silence when
everyone leaves you   alone

to confront the empty chair at breakfast
and everywhere in the house
where silence sits

no shoes kicked off at the front door
to snatch a still-warm cookie
then running off to play outdoors

Not the tolling of church bells
or even the filled pews
but the silence that surrounds you

[15] Published by Tower Poetry Society, Summer 2016. Volume 65, No. 1

[16] By Kathleen Norris

There are no words
for that kind of silence

Part 4
Good Grief

A Psalm - In the Darkness of Night

Barbara Heagy

Tonight, I speak of the unspeakable. How can I find the courage to face the blackness of my grieving soul full in the face?

The regrets, the lies, the things I didn't say, and the things I shouldn't have said while you were still alive. I was so harsh in my expectations, trapped in a web of my own making, because there were times I didn't have enough love and understanding to give you when you needed it most. And now death has taken you, and I will never have that chance again.

There were decisions I delayed or never made. I couldn't find the strength to make them and go down that dark path. Too weak and afraid, I ran from the responsibility. Others had to step in and convince me of choices my heart wasn't ready to face.

And now with the finality of death, I am filled with regret, anger, and shame. I am sick to death. It should have been me who went first, but I have been left behind, deserted and alone, to carry on with a life that has no meaning. I am a wretched case.

I can't face each day in a life that is too hard, for the guilt of never being strong enough, loving enough, or brave enough is becoming a burden I can no longer accept.

Better I be dead and in the ground beside you than live this life full of pain and suffering. I cannot bear it. I feel hopeless and doomed. The darkness of my soul consumes me, and my grief swallows me.

I suffer in guilt of the never-dids, the should-haves, and the never-wills. I sit each day and let it simmer as a festering sore in my heart.

Alone I sit in the shadows and hope at each day's end that I shall fall asleep into that eternal slumber that never wakens. I long for that relief. It would bring this never-ending trouble to a close and I would be free to join you. How much more can I bear?

How long must I wrestle with my thoughts
and day after day have sorrow in my heart?[17]

LORD my God, I called to you for help,
and you healed me.[18]

I have forgotten how to pray. I close my eyes and lie curled in the stillness of my hopelessness. My clenched fist holds the edges of the gaping wound. My heart is broken and sleep evades me. Rest is not to be mine.

Tonight I am weak and sick and no longer have the strength to hold on to this incessant agony that eats at me. I roll over and look out into the darkness. I call out to God, loosen my grip, and release the pain.

The dam breaks, and all my doubt, anger, fear and shame flows from my anguished soul in a flood that I can no longer

---

[17] Psalm 13:2 NIV

[18] Psalm 30:2 NIV

hold in.

I am free from the self-inflicted bonds of misery that held me prisoner in a tower of martyrdom. The floodgates are finally open and I am an empty vessel.

Into that wound, God pours his love and grace, filling the aching emptiness. Comfort and hope become my new companions. God's gentle hand begins its work, soothing the jagged edges of a heart held too long in captivity.

Understanding and joy are mine again. The open conduit of my broken heart becomes a healing pathway. God has the power to enter that which had been sealed. Goodness and clarity now make their way to mend the brokenness.

My soul is restored, forgiveness offered. I can forgive myself and believe and know that I am worthy of that great love and forgiveness.

I can begin to live and love again. I start with loving myself. With small, steady steps, I will find my way again.

I will move on, still missing you, but no longer hating myself. I am imperfect but I have been made perfect again by embracing my weaknesses. I will make changes in my life.

I am alive. I have a second chance to do better, be better and love better, for I am loved. I don't have to hold on to the pain or punish myself for surviving and believing that I honour you by holding on to my agony. I can pay tribute to you by living my life abundantly and with joy.

God will love me through others, for when they step forward—when I allow them in— their love, comfort and goodness will help me on my healing journey back to life again.

My armour was necessary for a time, to feel protected and closer to you, but it prevented me from being who I am, who I was meant to be. The barrier I put up kept me from letting goodness and love in.

Will I stop grieving? No. But if my heart is open, I will not suffer; the sorrow will not build up and consume me. I accept that you are gone. My memories and love for you will be pure and full of gratitude.

My grief will become like breathing—in and out. Inhale and exhale. Do I see exhaling as a negative action? No. It's just the natural release of air that I don't need anymore. My body has used it and now is freeing it so that the next healing breath can bring me new oxygen and life. Breathe—inhale, exhale—all part of the natural process of life.

You will always be with me, but I will begin to live again.

A Poem: 1 + 1 = 3

Barbara Heagy

You,
　Me,
Together make three.
A Venn diagram—
Two joined together
To create a third new one.
Two ones make an Us,
As unique
As the separates—
You and Me.
And how big the Us becomes
Depends on how close
The ones want to stand.
We had a lovely Us . . .
And now,
Now that you're gone,
Suddenly there's just Me again.
3 – 1 = 1

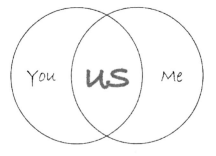

Tears

Barbara Heagy

That last hour as you lay dying, I stopped crying. Oh, I had my emotional breakdown when death stepped forward to let me know that it wasn't leaving without you. After that initial shock, once unbridled tears bolted from a reservoir of fear, I was able to compose myself. I found my place of acceptance and sat quietly holding your hand until death lightly picked you up in its gentle arms and carried you off silently into the night.

When I made that first phone call to my daughter, she told me she couldn't believe how calm my voice sounded. For the rest of that night, as last details unfolded, there was no more weeping.

It wasn't until I returned to bed that night, lying there without you, that the tears quietly began to flow once again. But this time, my daughter's strong, supporting fingers gripped mine with a steadfast love that held me up emotionally as they flowed from a deep well of sorrow.

As days passed, the tears would come, but most often I could choose when and where— alone in my car, in a corner of my garden, or in my lonely bed at night. There were times I couldn't choose; then they would leap with an "Aha!" like a hiding child appearing suddenly during a game of hide and seek. A smell, a gesture, a certain word spoken could trigger them and they would spurt out, causing me to gulp with a quick intake of air. But those tears were short-lived and quickly under control.

The most fearsome were the tears that came in waves— black, roiling water that crashed over me on a lonely shore. I never knew when to expect those. With them, there was no warning, no hint of their ominous presence. Those frothing tsunamis of grief would smash into me, leaving me shaking and sobbing even after their cold waters receded and returned to their oily depths once again.

With time, the tears came less and less, but they were always there. They still are. For the sorrow, the grief is always there. I never stop missing you, but I accept it. I have learned to move forward without you.

It's been five years now, and I still find myself crying. But I no longer regret the tears. They are a part of my strength and acknowledgement that you are never coming back. My tears come from the parts of you that can never be taken away, my treasured memories of all your goodness. It isn't all sadness. Sparkling memories of good times bring on bubbles of laughter and crinkled eyes too.

The laughter and tears, the joyful memories and painful despair, are all part of living a life without you. I embrace it all.

As much as I would never quell the merry mirth of you inside my soul, I would never quell my yearning for you. The acceptance of all my memories—the good and the bad, the joyful and sad—means I can live with it all. It's a vulnerable place, but it makes for an honesty and recognition that speaks of the truth of life, the yin and the yang.

I stand strong as the tears still roll down my face, and I stand strong with dimpled cheeks and effervescent laughter. I'm learning that tears aren't a weakness to be hidden. They acknowledge my true feelings and are a sign of bravery and understanding.

For this, after all, is life. And I am grateful for all of it.

A Different Walk

Donna Mann

"**M**y mother has gone back to her family ways, and I'd like to honour this even though it's not my understanding."

The woman's voice on the telephone was not familiar. Panic and fear was. This was obviously a daughter who wanted to respect her mother's heritage.

"My mother has chosen a different path to meet her creator. One with which I'm not familiar. Would you visit to listen, to follow her in these last days?"

The trembling in her voice presented a definite message of vulnerability.

I consented. Asking for the address, thinking it would be in the town in which I ministered, I took the directions she gave. The place was several miles into a district with which I was not familiar.

A tall, pleasant woman opened the door and welcomed me. She introduced me to several relatives, a few friends and to her husband. We sat at the kitchen table for a short time and I soon realized these people shared a deep care and love for this family. A realization that this was not my faith tradition, or understanding of life and death, gripped me.

In my mind's eye, I saw Jesus sitting on the edge of the well, in the strange country of Samaria—a foreign and sometimes hostile country. No, he wasn't lost. He was waiting.

"Could I meet your mother?" I asked the daughter.

She led me into a semi-darkened room, empty except for a large bed facing the door from which I'd entered. Behind the bed was a window covered with wooden venetian blinds.

"Mother, are you awake?" Her melodious voice resonated like a bird settling into a nest.

"Yes, I'm waiting." The raspy voice rattled in the room.

The daughter walked over to the bed, leaving me standing inside the room. "This is Donna. She's come to be with you during your time of preparation. I'll leave you now. The tea will be ready soon." She disappeared into the dimness of the room. I heard the click of the door behind me. I sat down on the chair beside her bed. The words of introduction dispelled my own fears of sharing this woman's journey. In the dimness of the room, I thought once again of Jesus sitting by the well... waiting.

"Dawn...a?" She dragged out the word, "Like the morning."

Silence.

"This is how I see you."

I hadn't thought she'd opened her eyes, even in her conversation with her daughter. The word 'wise' came to mind. I would learn something significant to help her walk the next step. In a lovely, gentle way, she told me how we would communicate, how our time together would be helpful.

I heard the squeak of the door and soon the daughter stood at her mother's bedside. She held medications in one hand, and a glass of water with a straw bobbing in the liquid in the other.

"I've brought your medication."

Covering her shoulder, in gentle laying-on-of hands, the daughter whispered, "God be with you, Mother, as you rest."

"Yes, this will be so."

Over the next three days, this little ritual between mother and daughter continued. The wise one, as I silently referred to her, took opportunity to speak of her faith in two or three words at a time, followed by silence. In some strange way, she appeared to be listening to receive the next selection of words to share with me.

I smiled, thinking how foolish it was to think I was helping her die. She was walking her path, word by word and I was falling in step.

Early one morning, the daughter phoned and told me her mother wanted me to come and take a few more steps with her.

Again, I sat in the familiar chair looking at the peaceful face of my wise friend. Without a greeting of any kind she said, "Thank you, Dawn... a for coming."

Silence.

"My time is near."

Silence.

"I will meet my Creator, soon." She chuckled. "Do not think the words, 'I'm sorry.'"

I looked closely at her. Yes, her eyes were watching me, like an owl that blinks and watches, blinks and watches.

"I'm at peace with you leaving this world," I said, and then I sighed. "I admit I will miss you."

"I will be with you in memory."

The daughter once again stood beside the bed with a glass of water and her pills.

"Just the water, please."

She gave her mother a drink.

"Will you read today?" the woman asked. I noticed several books on the side table.

"My daughter will bring my family and friends in to give me gifts to take on my journey." She paused and took a breath. "Some of what you hear or see may seem strange to you." She sighed. "I believe God has brought us both to the well of new life. Would you begin with your favourite passage from the Bible?"

My Bible, with all its bookmarks and highlighted phrases lay in my purse several feet away—out of reach. This Bible was old, King James version, unmarked, no colours and coloured papers, yet the pages were tattered as if it had been well used.

"What gives you strength will do the same for me."

Tears dropped on my cheeks and a few on my hands. If my chosen words would comfort her, we had reached a level of trust to bring us both to holy ground.

I chose a portion of Paul's letter to the Philippians from scraps of paper she'd handwritten and placed appropriately:

Finally, brothers and sisters, whatever is true, whatever is noble, whatever is right, whatever is pure...[19]

The Psalm was on a frayed page.

Yea, though I walk through the valley of the shadow of death. . .[20]

I read from one book, then another. Three, maybe four hours passed. Someone brought in tea and sandwiches, then a glass of water. Later someone brought in a crock of grape juice, a dish of grapes and small pieces of sweet bread. Sacrament of Communion!

As I continued to read, I glanced up to see several people surrounding the bed holding chunks of bread and small cups of juice. Candles flickered in various areas giving the room a peaceful appearance. In prayer, with eyes closed, I felt a movement of air in distinct rhythm.

The doctor entered, lowered his head to his patient and whispered. "Rest now, it won't be long before you'll go to your eternal rest."

---

[19] Philippians 4:8 KJV

[20] Psalm 23:4

He turned toward me and said, "Thank you for being here. You have walked the path with love."

My wise friend's laboured breathing filled the room.

"This is not about you, dear one. Just a few more steps. I am holding her hand. I will walk with her now."

No one had moved close, yet I knew the words were spoken to me.

I looked at her hands through my tears. They were lying palms up by her side. She was so ready and willing to leave this world.

Return, Oh Spring!

Ruth Smith Meyer

The morning dawns,
my consciousness aroused,
realizes its arrival
is cloudy, damp and cold.

My eyelids open slowly;
I pull the covers 'round.
It seems the clime has
my heart firmly in its hold.

Bleak February days
find echo in my heart.
Where are the sunshine,
warmth and loving grace,

the shape and meaning,
hopes and dreams,
the touch, the feel, and sight
of my dear one's face?

Oh come, warmth and touch
of Eternal Spring,
melt grief's ice and snow,
disperse winter's chill,

and in the warming trickle
of the certain thaw,
soak the earth of promise

that lies beneath it still;

awaken slumbering seeds
and initiate new growth
of love and life,
in altered and innovative cast.

Emerging from the earth,
facing toward the sun,
may hopes and dreams
return to me at last.

Down the Road of Grief I Go

Ruth Smith Meyer

In the first months after the death of my husband, Norman, I found that time had no meaning anymore. My memory was no longer dependable. The configuration of life had changed so drastically that there seemed to be no anchor posts to a sense of direction. It felt like I was driving through a deep winter fog with snow blanketing the road, the ditches and fences. There was nothing to show me where the road was, and yet I had to travel on and on.

I so desperately felt the need for a guidepost along the way. God's love came now and then, through the assurance that someone still cared and also missed my loved one. It came when someone called with encouragement in a lonely evening, and when I was reminded that a familiar task still awaited when the ability to fulfill it returned. To this life-long

reader, it startled me to realize I could read whole pages of books—even the Bible—and not comprehend a word I had read.

Throughout my life, I'd often felt excited about changes, although I also had an accompanying sense of anxiety as well. Those usually were changes that I felt enthusiastic about. The death of my husband plunged me into a change I did not plan for or desire. I was thrust into circumstances I had not chosen. There existed no way out—no way but ahead. I had to journey through—whether I wanted to or not.

A whole new set of overwhelming challenges faced me—dealing with a big hole, a stripping away. An important support on which I had depended disappeared with Norman's demise, as did also the focus for my love.

The death of my dear life-partner caused an upset in my routine of living—in the basic concepts by which I had lived. It was traumatic because its consequences were so comprehensive. Those not closely involved didn't seem to 'get' the enormity the loss had on my life.

Peggy Anderson, the author of *Wife after Death*, with whom I took the course called Alone and Growing, says that often it is the bereft person who has to be the educator about grieving. However, too often, it is easier for the grieving to outwardly respond in the way that is thought to be the norm, rather than to reveal the depth and length of their grief.

People want to believe that a few weeks or months will get the main part of grieving done. So after a few months, those who have suffered loss start hiding their feelings because they begin sensing it is unacceptable to share their grief anymore. The myths are therefore self-perpetuating. I felt that pressure myself but was determined to be honest and open. I sometimes wished to restore the custom of wearing black for the first year after the death of a family member. It had some advantages. It reminded people that grief was ongoing, that the bereft person needed time.

Many people who stand by are afraid of talking about the death and feeling of loss; they are afraid it may make the person hurt all the more or, heaven forbid, make them cry! Shakespeare penned these lines, "Give sorrow words: the grief that does not speak whispers to the o'er fraught heart, and bids it break." When I read that, my heart blessed the old bard for understanding.

One of the most valuable gifts very few people gave to me

was the gift of truly listening and letting me cry when that was needed. For a time, I even paid a counsellor to listen. For me, part of the process of healing was talking about it.

After Norman died, I often felt like one horse in a two-horse hitch. Everything seemed off-centre and odd. Nothing pulled evenly. I found that it isn't a case of "getting over it" as much as finding a way to go on and learning to live with it.

Fresh grief affects every waking hour; there is such an aura of unreality and confusion. One feels so lost. As time passes, there are glimpses of better times ahead, more acceptance of life as it is now. At first, those times are fleeting, but eventually, they come for longer periods. However, it takes only small happenings to crumble any progress you think you have achieved.

Each of these occurrences brings a fresh wave of grief washing over us. Like a sandcastle, broken down by sun and incoming tide, new beginnings and fresh courage are washed away. It's then we find we need to peel the next layer of grief. There is a saying, "Life is like an onion, you peel it layer by layer, and sometimes you weep." But with each layer, I came closer to the centre which holds the real essence of life—the place where God dwells, where I could be in harmony with him and myself.

God was right there, if I stopped to hear and feel him— walking hand-in-hand with me, crying with me in my sadness, holding me in those loving arms, and sometimes, when I was too tired and worn to even acknowledge Him, he carried me.

One morning, sometime after Norman's death, I was faced with several tasks for which he usually took responsibility. I felt so inadequate. At my age, the possibility of how many years I might have to live alone stretched stark and bleak ahead of me.

In my morning quiet time, my whole being called out to God. "I trust you, but I just can't understand how you think I can manage without Norman." Tears streamed down my cheeks. "I just don't understand God, I just don't understand!"

Suddenly, I felt lifted up, as though I had been put on the very lap of my Lord and I heard a gentle, kind and loving voice. "I know you don't understand." Those words, even without answers, made such a difference.

I wasn't alone in my cries. The Psalmist often cried out in his frustration and grief. He told God very honestly and succinctly, just what he thought of the turns his life had taken, the pits of loneliness and despair in which he landed. It was often in these shed tears of the psalmist—in the pouring out of his despair— that he became aware of the solidarity of God's goodness and mercy. And so it was for me.

Yes, I did find comfort in knowing God's care, but I also found something else to be true that I had read. Raymond R. Mitsch and Lynn Brookside wrote in *Grieving the Loss of Someone You Love,* "even though Christ is always beside us, walking with us through the storm, we mustn't fall into the trap of believing that our awareness of Christ's presence is all we need. This is simply not so. God created us to be in fellowship with others of our kind. We aren't being immature Christians, 'disloyal' to God, or ungrateful, when we openly acknowledge that we need to be comforted by friends and family."

A very real part of grief is the desire to go back to what life used to be—to hang on to what was. Gerald Sittser, who, in a moment lost his wife, daughter, and mother in one car accident, had a dream. He saw the sun setting in front of him, and behind him, the frightening darkness looming. He began to frantically run west, trying desperately to catch the sun, to remain in its fiery warmth and light. He was losing ground and found himself in the twilight with the darkness catching up to him. He collapsed to the ground and fell into despair, feeling he would live in the darkness forever.

Sittser told the dream to his sister and she pointed out to him that the quickest way for anyone to reach the sun and the light of day is not to run west, chasing after the setting sun, but to head east, plunging into the darkness until one comes to the sunrise.

That insight was confirmed by the 'vision' I had experienced shortly after Norman's death. I found myself standing at a white gate, surrounded by banks of lovely flowers, bathed in light. It seemed to be like the gates I had walked to with Norman in his final moments. I had felt the same glory there.

Now I felt God nudging me away from those gates onto a path that led into a huge, dark forest. As I stepped into that dense forest, I felt the coolness and shivered. It was so dark, I could not see. I dreaded taking the path, yet knew in my heart I must go on. As I groped my way along the path, I could barely see a step ahead. I had to test and feel the next step with my feet.

Gradually, my eyes became accustomed to the darkness, and I became aware of interesting patterns and fauna on the forest floor. A voice whispered, "Do not hurry through, but learn to appreciate the darkness and the growth in this environment." In obedience, I found beauty and security there and became more comfortable with the darkness. God's Spirit became more real.

After a while the path started going upward, becoming rough and at times dangerous, with steep rocks on one side, a narrow path and sharp drop on the other. Sometimes, there were tricky corners around rocky outcrops. Slight fear and trepidation were dispelled when I sensed that an angel hovered over me and protected me from danger. Sometimes I had to climb over fallen trees or piles of rocks. The climb became quite steep.

Eventually, the trees became less dense, bits of light shone through, and the path became smoother. After some time, the path was not so steep, and suddenly, I came into a clearing high on the mountain. Looking back, I could see the tops of the trees through which I had travelled. What a difference in perspective, when seen from the top instead of underneath!

The clearing was not large, and I could see valleys and other sizeable hills ahead, but for now, I rested in the sunny meadow, blue skies above, and watched eagles soaring among the scattered clouds. I felt at peace and somehow a different, more mature person, integrating what was and what is, into a new whole. Seeds of hope were born within me that day.

This vision proved to be quite accurate in the next period of my life. The remembrance gave me hope that new meaning and direction would come.

Visions of Gifts, Gaps and New Growth

Ruth Smith-Meyer

Mental pictures often help me in the crisis times of my life. In the moments after the departure of Norman's spirit, another vision presented itself to me. There was my beautifully completed package of marriage to Norman. I saw it as having been an empty box at the beginnng of our marriage.

We had carefully filled the space item by item. Yes, some seemed like mistakes or less than the best choices, but each item was necessary to complete the package. Everything was packed and neatly arranged; now the box was full.

In the last months, we had put in the last few thoughtful items, then we worked at the wrapping to make it a beautiful package indeed. The last hours were like the ribbon and bow and gift card. Now it was complete, beautiful, and deeply satisfying, ready to give to our Maker. No regrets or might-have-beens—except perhaps a longing that it could have been a bigger package.

Wonderful and utterly moving as that moment was, I also felt as though a large part of me was gone when that package was given to the Master, as though I had suffered an amputation—a great loss.

With Norman's passing from this life to the next, it seemed as though we'd both left the existence to which we were accustomed. He went to the presence of his Maker but I, too, moved to a different kind of living—a life without Norman. Some of the same 'furnishings' were there, but many of our usual rituals and our plans for the future were no longer applicable to me as a single person. I would have to shop around for new fittings that would answer my present needs. As part of that search I wrote the following poem:

Of Blooms and Blooming On

The colour in our life
together
had burst forth
in beauteous tones of bright splendour,
emerged from the dark earth of friction
that refines and breaks down
to fertile soil.

The comfort and joy in our
togetherness
sent forth tangible perfume
that wafted through everything we touched,
partook of,
enjoyed,
so that even others stopped
to deeply inhale and smile in pleasure.

Came the call ending our
togetherness,
too soon,
far too soon.

Savouring the moments,
we clung to time for a while;
blessing and being blessed,
loving and being loved
and in the end, releasing.

From the purest centre of our love
together
we let go,
to go on blooming.
You to ethereal heights and nebulous form,
I, taking on a darker hue
of muted beauty,
in a world bereft of you.

Still I try to let go,
to grow and bloom
to release the fragrance
of love once known
and still living in my heart.

Framed, along with a picture I drew depicting the parting, that poem hangs on my wall ready to encourage me, to help me let go and to find ways I can still bloom and let beauty shine on me and through me—even the second time around.

Missing Mum
Alan Anderson

When I was younger I thought my parents would live forever. That belief ended with the death of my father a number of years ago. It was totally destroyed with the death of my mother. When Mum was alive, I couldn't imagine what my life would be without her. Her death reminded me that life is a journey and grief is part of it.

When Mum was in hospital shortly before she died, I had to face the fact that perhaps her life would soon wind down. A doctor had warned her of the possibility she could experience a massive stroke. When she told me of this, I believed her. Although it wasn't something I wanted to hear, I accepted it. I regret not asking her how she was feeling about that possibility. Perhaps I was more focused on how I would miss her. Without mum, there would be a hole in my life that would never be filled.

Just a mere couple of days after Mum came home from the hospital, I received a phone call from one of my brothers. It was a call I expected, yet dreaded. By the time my wife and I arrived at my brother's home, Mum had died. A policeman was already at my brother's home and an ambulance would arrive shortly after with the coroner.

I went into her room to see her. I thought, "Perhaps she's only unconscious." I wanted just a few more minutes with her. My mind was swimming. I was talking to myself, saying things like, "Not now, Mum! Stay with us just a bit longer!" I soon realized, however, she was indeed dead.

The ambulance guys had left Mum lying on the floor in her bedroom. I wished they could have picked her up and laid her on her bed. I thought to myself, "Would they have left their mothers on the floor?"

I sat on the floor beside her. It was just the two of us in the room. I looked her in the face and talked to her, even though I knew she could no longer respond. I remember saying to her that I was sorry I didn't get to her before she died. I asked her to open her eyes. I said, "Hey Mum, it's Alan," as if that was going to make a difference. My grief was dictating the words I was saying. My mind was swirling and I thought I was going to pass out. At this point I was trying not to cry and I don't know why. At the same time, however, tears were stinging my eyes.

I knew she was dead, but my heart didn't want to let her go. I wished I could take care of her and make her better. My mind, in an instant, took me back to when I was a little boy. I remember when I was sick and Mum took care of me. She seemed to know what I needed at the time. All I needed was to know she was there for me. I grieved that I hadn't been there for her in her last minutes. I told Mum I loved her and kissed her on her forehead. I held her hand then told her goodbye.

Loving someone deeply means you will also grieve deeply. That was my experience. I'm not sure if you really can prepare yourself for the death of someone so loved. For me, grief was profoundly emotional.

My sadness was raw and the intensity of my grief surprised me. I remember wanting to be by myself in order to scream my head off. It was like the cognitive me was fighting with the emotional me. I thought in the moment I had to be strong for my family, yet I wanted to bawl my eyes out.

The coroner told me he would be removing my mum's body from the house soon. I went downstairs to the basement so I wouldn't see her leaving. One of my sons and his wife were with me.

They asked if I was okay. I remember saying something like, "My mum's dead!" It hit me hard! I couldn't believe I said it.

"My mum's dead!"

I turned around toward the front door only to see what I dreaded. The coroner's assistants carried Mum's body, wrapped in a body bag. They took her away. I remember falling onto a chair and crying like I haven't cried for years.

I embraced my grief and allowed it to wash over me. The grief I felt and expressed was a new pain. It was as if my soul would fly away leaving me completely and emotionally empty and alone. My grief taught me that to experience the death of parents was a profoundly intense pain beyond measure. In my experience, at least, it's not something I could have prepared myself for.

The people I call "my teachers" in life, including my Mum, have taught me many things about grief over the years.

One of the things they have taught me was that it's a process where there is no closure. Dr. Kenneth Doka, in his book, *Grief Is A Journey: Finding Your Path Through Loss*, states, "...Grief is not about letting go of past relationships or closing yourself off from them. Even in bereavement you continue your bond—albeit in a different way." I am thankful there is no closure. I am glad I have not been released from the memories of my mother, including the memories of how her death affected me.

My memories of life with my mother are alive and well. I guess this is one way in which someone never truly dies. When I'm with family, I often tell stories of what Mum was like. I remember things she liked and loved. Now and again, when we may be having family dinners, my siblings and I often recount memories of both parents. When I make homemade soup, I recall that Mum loved to make soup for the family as well. Making soup also brings a smile to my face, because although mum loved to make us soup, she never ate it herself. She, in fact, didn't like her soup. I always thought that was a bit odd because her soup tasted delicious.

My memories of my parents, and especially of my mother, help keep me grounded as I make my way through life. I have learned to try to be patient with other people. I often observed how my mother approached difficult people.

She would state her opinion of a matter and leave it at that, and she also didn't become embroiled in other people's business. In other words, she would not meddle in their affairs. It was like she lived according to a Bible teaching.

Like one who grabs a stray dog by the ears is someone who rushes into a quarrel not their own[21]

I try to live that way as well.

We are never free from our grief. It does not define who we are, yet it remains embedded within us. I know I will never see my mother again in this life. I have come to grips with this both emotionally and intellectually. In spite of my mother's death, my relationship with her remains, only it is different now. My grief remains, although not with the intensity it once had. I will never get over my grief. There is no complete release from it—there is no closure.

At Mum's memorial service, the family gathered to bid our final and fondest farewell to her at the local cemetery. It was a fairly pleasant day for February. The weather cooperated by not drenching us with the rain common to the Lower Mainland of British Columbia. It was cool enough for

---

[21] Proverbs 26:17 NIV.

jackets, but at least it wasn't freezing. The trees stood naked, waiting for the warmth of spring to come and clothe them again, just as Mum had clothed us when we were children after our baths. The evergreens close by sheltered us from the cool breeze, a bittersweet reminder that Mum will never shelter us again.

Almost nine years have gone by since Mum died. There are no more phone calls from her on my birthday. I saved the tape of her last birthday phone call to me. Somehow, to this day, I can't bring myself to listen to it.

Over the years, I still think of her calling me. I imagine her asking if I am having a good birthday. She would say something like she would see me soon. I can hear her asking how the grandkids are doing. She would ask if my wife and I are going out for dinner to celebrate.

I think of Mum often and miss her with an ache in my heart. Perhaps as part of my grief journey, it is an ache I want to keep. I also remember Mum's smile and her wonderful, almost girlish, laugh. I never want to lose that memory either. It makes me smile and fills me with hope.

A Beautiful Death

Glynis M Belec

"**I**f I want to die, I jolly well will die!"

Mum remained a feisty British beauty until her dying day. She liked to be in charge at all times, so Mum's response to my brother John's desire—to find her a doctor who could do something—was not a surprise.

Mum had come to terms that her time was fast approaching. She wasn't the least bit scared, and it was wonderful to hear her 'communing with angels' or 'chatting with God' over her last two weeks of life.

For Mum's safety, we had placed a monitor system in her room so we could hear if she was in trouble, or if she was calling to go to the bathroom. There was something perfectly reassuring as I sometimes overheard Mum's words. A peaceful calm, a tender knowing, a quiet concentration permeated and assured me she was ready to take her final step in life. Death.

Mum had been living with us for over six months. It had become too much for Dad to care for her, so they decided, and my husband and I agreed, that she would move in with us. So she did. It was hard for both Mum and Dad after 53 years of marriage. I recall one phone call Mum made to Dad.

She was crying and telling Dad how much she missed him. My eyes filled with tears as I heard Mum speak in her frail voice telling him how much she wished she could come home to be with him. Being privy to this tender conversation made my tears spill, and I started to wonder if we had made the correct decision. Then the conversation continued.

"I really do want to come home, but I know I can't. This is my home now." My heart hurt.

"It's the time that we knew would come, Lou. I am grateful to be here and not in a nursing home. Let's just remember what we had and we will both manage."

I walked away. And wiped my trickling tears.

Two weeks later, the family gathered at Mum's bedside. She was failing fast. She knew it and that's why she had asked to see everyone—"Quickly," she had said.

Mum wanted all her children there. And just as she had her way in life, we would give it to her in death, too. Dad. Rosemary. Glynis. Susan. John. Some of the extended family came, too. Family was paradise on this side of heaven to Mum, so it was fitting that so many came. Mom hung on and sang songs. We made a recording of Mum reciting poetry, singing, talking to her loved ones, who didn't know whether to laugh or cry. We did both.

Mum was a joker. She insisted on reciting her poem about 'men' that she had made up and we all giggled. Evening arrived and Mum was still hanging on. One by one, we got to lay beside her in her comfy hospital-type bed. When it was my turn, I felt like a little girl all over again cuddling next to my precious mother after a bad dream.

The sun set that evening, but Mum was not quite ready. Dad was getting tired. We set him up on a cot next to Mum and everyone else 'kipped' where they could. It was a restless sleep for most—except Mum. She snored—for one last night on this earth. We had complained often over the years about Mum's loud snoring. But that night no one said a word. Instead, we drank it in.

The next day was different. Mum was weak and didn't say much. Her usual good appetite had waned and she barely ate any porridge for breakfast. We let Mum sleep for a while. She awoke just a little before noon.

"What would you like for lunch, Mum?"

I was prepared to go to the ends of the earth to make Mum her last meal. It didn't matter what she would ask for, I would get it. Roast beef with Yorkshire puddings and gravy? That's what I expected.

In barely a whisper, Mum said, "I would like pizza, strawberry mousse and a cup of tea." We all laughed as I reiterated her order.

"I'm serious," she whispered.

We knew better than to try to talk our mother out of anything, even on her death bed. And so we ordered pizza. I whipped up some strawberry mousse and someone put the kettle on.

Mum could barely chew the pizza that my sister was feeding to her. We could tell by the gentle sounds she was making that she was enjoying the flavours, although she ended up spitting out most of it. She seemed to really enjoy the strawberry mousse. Then she got to her tea. Mum loved her tea. She sipped it delicately.

Then her last words, "Hurry!"

We weren't sure if she meant 'hurry with the tea' or if she was speaking about haste for another reason. Mum closed her eyes for the last time.

We thought she had breathed her last, but she drifted for almost two hours. Very close to the end, she took a deep breath. The whole family cried in unison.

Then her breathing resumed. We all sighed, knowing we had a little more time with our beautiful Mum. It happened again. She inhaled deeply and we thought she was gone. We all cried again.

Three more times. It was like our jokester Mum was doing it on purpose. She would have loved that. Oh, how she loved to tease and laugh and play jokes. But this was no joke.

Mum took her final breath, surrounded by her loved

ones.

I couldn't bear the thought of losing my mother, but the day had come. My mind flashed back to the letter I wrote to both my parents when I was a little child—imploring them to never, ever die because I could never live without them. I was grown up now, but my heart still felt as if a piece of it had been ripped away, and I wondered how I would ever live without my Mum.

It's been almost ten years since Mum died. I know she is with Jesus so that brings great comfort to this little-girl heart, and I look forward to a great reunion one day.

Meanwhile, I have her sweater. When my heart aches for Mum, I pull it out. I tug it over my head and I find somewhere quiet. And I cry. Then I hear her voice.

"I jolly well was ready to die and you knew that. Wipe away those tears. You also know I love you very much. Now go do something useful. And who said you could wear my sweater?"

Part 5
Learning Through Loss

Grief Has Taught Me
Barbara Heagy

Over six years ago, my second husband, Tom, was diagnosed with terminal cancer and died seven months later. He was the love of my life, a true soul mate. The day of his death, and many of those within the subsequent years, have been among the most difficult days of my life. The initial grief was devastating and crushing; my very being was shattered, my heart ripped open. Yet, when I was willing to look deeply at that gaping hole of grief, slowly but surely, grief took me on a convoluted path that led to a new me. It taught me about who I am, about life and death, and helped me find new meaning and purpose in life. I have been transformed, never to be the same.

Grief taught me about itself. It is one of the most powerful emotions I have ever experienced. I have always prided myself on being a strong woman. In the face of past adversity, I would be tough, work hard, gather up my personal strength and rise above my challenges, undefeated. This was different.

In those first numbing, fog-filled days after Tom's death, grief lived outside of my body. It was immense, long-lasting, and with a life of its own, attacking suddenly and unexpectedly. One night as I lay in bed, it came like a giant ocean wave breaking upon my memories and love for Tom. I sank into the depths of it until it washed away, leaving me dripping and breathless on the shore.

Grief had its triggers that could leave me reeling and out of control. Two months after Tom died, I was back working at my full-time job as an elementary school teacher. I was in the gym supervising a group of children who were watching the movie *Up* which had been one of our favourites.

The couple in the movie had always reminded Tom and me of ourselves. As I watched them and their on-screen affection, I began to weep and moved to the back of the dark gym so the children couldn't see me wiping the tears from my eyes.

Six months later, grief continued to surprise me. I was walking by our wedding picture hanging on the wall in the hallway and threw Tom a quick kiss. "Hi, honey." And just as quickly, a painful sob broke free, as sharp grief hit me with a slap across the heart. The suddenness and unexpectedness of it left me shaking.

I learned that grief comes in stages. At first, it was Tom and his presence I was missing. All my focus was outwards on him. I was bound to him, mooning over him, crying over him, holding on to what we had together. I was living in the past. Then after five months, I began to change. It was sinking deeper—the realization that he was never coming back—and I had my own full life ahead of me, without him. And a new kind of grief began.

At nine months, I wrote in my journal:
I dream of you less and less, but think of you more and more. But it's not really you I'm thinking of. It's the life without you that is starting to surface. What once felt unreal is now becoming reality. I'm beginning to accept the fact that you will never be in my life again. And I try to imagine what that

life will be like. In this next kind of grief, I must move on without you.

I have learned that grief doesn't come in nice, tidy stages. It has a twisting path that goes in and out of healing and new growth and back into emotional outbursts, anger, and panic. I may think I'm doing just fine and then something will happen that makes me realize I really am not as fine as I thought.

At ten months, I decided to visit a friend, Charlie, who owned a local variety store near where I worked. He and his wife, Judy, had been a part of my life for over twenty years. They knew my children well and had been happy when they heard of my marriage to Tom. I had told them of Tom's cancer diagnosis, but I couldn't face them with the news of Tom's death without breaking down.

Finally, one Friday night after work, I decided I could do it. I stayed and talked with Charlie for a while, talking in between customers, catching him up on the year's news. I did manage to tell him without an emotional outburst. Until I got back into my car and began the long drive home. The tears began and I had to pull over.

"Oh, life is so hard." I screamed at God. "Why has this happened to me? If this is some sort of big master plan, then I hate it! Why me? Why did you take away something that was so good, God?"

A little voice whispered. "This has nothing to do with whether you deserve it or not. Death is a part of life for all of us, for all of nature. It happens to all of us sooner or later. And there is an element of chance to it all as well as an element of consequences for the choices we make and how we live our lives. And there is an element of God moving through our lives with purpose too. Rest in God's arms and move on with trust."

There's a saying, "Time will heal" in the grieving process, but I have learned that it's not completely true. I used to count the months, thinking that, with time, things would get better.

At seven months, I still grieved. I could still cry uncontrollably at times. Some of my biggest moments of dismay came when I met those who had lost loved ones. One year, three years, sixteen years later, they still grieved and cried aloud when they thought of their loved one. It's been six years for me, and I can still tear up thinking of Tom.

But it's no longer a raw, open wound. There is a scar, but the pink healed flesh of my broken heart holds the wound closed for the most part.

As my focus moved from the loss of Tom to my future without him, my grieving changed. I could no longer hold on to the old role model of who I was.

When I was filling out all the paperwork for Tom's estate, I often had to check the box "Single" or "Married." I told Lara, my daughter, that they needed a "Widowed" box. I didn't feel single, but I knew I was no longer married.

I began to ask myself new questions: Who am I? What's life all about? What is my purpose? It took time, but I began to redefine my identity and create a new life. I spent more time with family and friends. As I began to learn more about myself and the world around me, I read books, articles, watched videos and documentaries on death, dying and grief. I sought new knowledge about creativity and self-development and began to ask myself what was really important to me. Joining the YMCA was a good start with regular exercise as part of my routine. I joined a writer's club and a photography club, and then wrote and self-published a book about my life with Tom.

I stopped being a victim of grief and looked it full in the face. Grief became less fearful as I learned that I was big enough and strong enough to face the pain and survive.

The pain is still there when I think of Tom, but I will keep feeling it, for I would rather remember him with tears than not remember him at all. Looking at the pictures and sharing stories about him may make me cry, but it is a bitter sweetness.

How wonderful it is to hold all the precious memories of him and linger over the moments we had together. Each tear is a prism full of all the colours of Tom.

I talked to others, heard their grief stories and together we shared our wisdom and understanding. I have come to realize that life is precious and valuable, not to be wasted. I am filled with gratitude for life's many gifts. Even the painful ones.

For I have learned that it is in the depths of despair that sometimes the greatest change can take place. From dark, deep roots come the sweet, green growth of new life.

Ever Shadow

Barbara Heagy

You, my shadow,
I feel you close.
I look
And see your outline.
You move with me,
Ever-connected,
Ever-one.

I tread lonely paths
And feel your presence
Walking along with me.
I stop. You too.
My second skin,
Ever-present,
Ever-bonded.

A crowded street before me,
With strangers' faces.
You are a broken shadow
Scattered disjointedly
Over their heads,
Ever-stretching,
Ever-places.

In the quiet,
I turn the pages of my book,
Our fingers together.
I question and hear your answer,
An echo from the past,

Ever-knowing,
Ever-felt.

Those rare times
When light shines
A direct beam to my soul,
It casts no shadow.
Where then?
Deep inside,
You're wrapped around my soul.
Ever-within,
Ever-mine.

To a Grieving Friend

Barbara Heagy

Dear Friend,

Thank you for your message and comments about my husband's cancer journey and subsequent death. My story is a sad one; we all have our sad stories, but I am grateful for the great love of my husband, Tom, and his incredible spirit that insisted on living every day, even when he was dying. Our experience taught me great life lessons.

We all are dying. Not one of us will escape that end to our lives. Tom and I both embraced life, held our precious lives closer to us than ever before. We all should live like that every day, for none of us knows when our end is near. Don't wait for a terminal cancer diagnosis, ill health, or the natural physical deterioration of our bodies as we age. When I was left alone, I accepted it. For some reason, unbeknownst to me, God decided to take Tom early in our marriage. I was to be alone for this time in my life. And I grieved. Grief would come in silently and unexpectedly and hit me like a giant wave, leaving me shaken and cold on a lonely shore. The first year was the hardest because, as I began to realize, I had to go through every holiday, every celebration, every season, every special day without Tom. But the waves stopped enveloping me, and I was able to breathe through them as time passed.

I still miss him. I still cry at unexpected times. But I keep moving forward for I have been given the gift of life and I don't want to squander it. I want to know that when I come to the end of my life, I have asked myself, "Who are you? What are your passions? What are you curious about? What do you want to do or say before your good life is gone?" I sought love and companionship with my family and friends.

I began to think of my own desires of my heart; I asked myself what I wanted to experience and accomplish with my life before I die. I travelled, sometimes alone. I joined a writer's club and a photography club too. I sought new friendships, new experiences and decided to write a book.

Every morning is a new beginning, a day to be grateful for, a day to do all things that bring joy and satisfaction. We can choose to dwell in our sorrows and losses, or we can choose to seek joy and think about new experiences.

You are a strong and educated woman with many interests, it seems. I am sure there were times that you wanted to do special things in your life that in the past you just didn't have the time or circumstances to do them.

I, for one, always wanted to write a book, but with working full-time and raising three children, I didn't have that time to sit for long periods to contemplate my life, as I do now. When Tom was in my life, I gave him time, because I wanted to. I sat through many football games and hockey games on TV because it meant we could do it together. Now I don't. I read more books and spend more time with my family and friends.

What have you always wished you had more time for? What have you always wanted to do, but haven't done yet? What new thing do you want to learn?

It's been such a short time since you lost your husband. Just getting through a normal day is not an easy thing. Be easy on yourself. You're doing well. In time, the pain will lessen and you'll get through it. You have been brought to this planet as a one-of-a-kind, unique individual. This is a time to focus on you. Don't be afraid to reach out to others for support, companionship, and love. Bit by bit, you will become stronger, more thankful for your own life, and the opportunities to explore all your dreams and hopes. It probably doesn't feel that way right now at all, but it will come. You have done a good thing by reaching out and being so honest and sincere with sharing your story. That is a strong step forward.

Warmly,
Barbara

Grief
Donna Mann

Don't think you can forget about it and it'll go away. It won't.

Don't think you can go on without finishing what you've begun. You can't.

Don't think you'll lose memories of your loved one. You won't.

Don't think you can complete your grief in isolation. You can't.

Don't think you can manage after a loss without managing your grief first. You guessed it!

(A poem scribbled among my papers probably written in the late 70s).

Grief's Hold
Donna Mann

I am contained within walls without doors
Even if I see an opening I do not want to leave
to move toward the light.
nor would I know how
for I have no desire or strength to open it,
each part is like stone.
Immovable
limiting
and restraining

In this place of my spirit
there is no give and take,

no pulse or rhythm
no life or warmth
no room to move around
or look beyond

I see only straight lines, secrets and seals
and feel only stagnation, stillness, and scourge.
Here I wear sackcloth and ashes
I have no energy to lift a hand
or feel my heartbeat.

Grief paralyzes, immobilizes, scrutinizes
Yet in time
I feel it changing me.
becoming a gift
that will set me free.
I begin to understand,
it yields to me
to help me move on.

*(I wrote this poem in my journal in the 70s. It evolved and later was
printed in WinterGrief (2003). As I have come to understand grief more
deeply, this revision continues to define my experience.)*

Christmas isn't Merry Anymore
(Millie's Song)
Donna Mann

I sat in a hospital ward beside a man who'd spent too long at the local bar. It'd obviously been his habit for many years, as he didn't seem remorseful.

Silently I wished he'd leave, but I tried to make small talk for the sake of the patient. His wife, someone I'd recently met, lay in the bed before us. For some weird reason, he seemed to think he would bring his wife the spirit of Christmas by his presence. He kept saying between hiccups,

"Merry Christmas darlin.'"

His efforts to give her some joy on this Christmas Eve had gone awry. She turned her face away from him, perhaps to avoid his stale-smelling breath more than anything else.

How did I get into this marital dilemma? It serves me right, I suppose, since I'd let my name stand for on-call in Emergency on Christmas Eve. He hadn't meant to hurt her, he said, wiping the drool from his mouth. "She's my honey."

Within the hour, his snoring covered any conversation I tried to have with his wife. She was dying, she'd been sick for a long time. Had wanted to die for a long time. Had apparently wanted to escape one more Christmas.

As she had grown sicker, his drinking had increased. Heaven only knows how much he was suffering.

From what I gathered, their life together had been toxic from the beginning. She had suffered through three miscarriages, and they'd both agonized through their three-year-old's long illness ending in death.

That was many years before, and both parents had lost sight of love since then. But I didn't think she would die tonight, although she might have given her life to manage it.

The name on the bed-sign said 'Millie' in large black letters. I wanted to gain this woman's trust. I wanted to know her as a friend, even in the short time we might have together. However, there was little trust between us, and less time to make it happen.

I sat through the long night, and after listening to her, a melody in a minor key continued to float through my mind. Then the words came one after another. I wished I had a guitar or piano so I could hear this song. More than that, I wanted to sing it to her. But, that would not happen tonight.

Her breath eased in and out, almost to the rhythm of the song. Or was I thinking the words to match the cadence of her breathing? In some transcendent way, the song seemed to belong to her; I was only the one to bring it into reality.
I went home after my shift and felt called to return to sit with Millie the next night.

Christmas carols played somewhere in the distance. Maybe it was carollers coming in from the street to share their music.

Suddenly, her voice soft and sad, resonated through the melody of the carols. "Christmas has never been joyful for us."

I almost missed those words.

I knew she was including her husband, even though again tonight, he snored as he slumped in the chair. "Silent night, Holy night. Christmas has never been silent or holy." She sighed and moved her face toward me. "And Christmas has never been merry, as some of them sing." She turned away. "And Christmas was always merry for him." She glanced quickly to the side.

I sat, listening.

"We never had a family, tried but…. Never even had a

pet. Just us, and that was one of many mistakes we made in our life."

I looked at her and wondered about the number of other families torn apart during this time of year. She grieved the loss of love, family and friendship. Maybe more than anything, she grieved the loss of her husband to alcohol, so many years before. Yet, in some distorted way, he loved her. And she obviously still loved him.

"I'm glad you're here tonight…and I'm glad Mike's here too." Her voice whispered the words. "And maybe the songs of Christmas will…"

Two hours of silence filled the room before slow beeps began. A nurse came quietly into the room to close the curtain.

Christmas Isn't Merry Anymore(Millie's Song)

Words And Music By Donna Mann

Notation By Louise Elder

Vs1: I would like to be with you at Christ- mas time

I would like to share your lone- li- ness and find

mist- le- toe to hang and bells to ring

Go to mid- night church and car- ols sing.

Vs2: If your mem' ries aren't so good then bor- row mine

Ones of love 'n shar- in' 'round those folks for whom you care.

Some- times grief and heart- ache smo- ther all that's good,

- 1 -

created with iWriteMusic

Christmas Isn't Merry Anymore(Millie's Song)

Robs what once was mer- ry ____ from folks 'n gifts 'n food.____

Vs3:
If you can't have Christ- mas like you used to have 'n

do the things that made the sea- son grand

Fill your bro- ken heart with dreams and good mem- o- ries____ Let

Je- sus bring the ho- ly to your heart,_____ Let

good- ness in your Christ- mas be the start._____

created with iWriteMusic

After the Night.

Ruth Smith Meyer

L ife dealt
a crushing blow-
You picked me up
and held me close.
I felt your arms
but could not see
your face.

Where was your face
just when I needed
to see it most?
I cried
and lay exhausted
and cried again
until I was spent.

Finally, my grief
began to ease.
Like a child catching
a shuddering breath,
I raised my head
from the succour of your shoulder,
the warmth of your neck,

…and there, so close to mine,
beheld your loving face.

Photo: Glynis M Belec

Sprouting New Growth

Ruth Smith Meyer

"**D**on't waste a good difficulty through not growing by it," is a phrase I repeated many times over the years.

That phrase haunted me through Norman's illness and death and in the days after. Sometimes I wished I had never said it in the first place, much less repeated it. After a while though, I felt God was telling me, "You know how much it blessed others by openly sharing, through *Marriage Encounter*, the difficult and growing times of your marriage. Now you have something else you need to share. Other people need to hear it." I wasn't so sure, yet I couldn't ignore that little voice.

When an opportunity arose to share my journey, I shared the details of death and grief with fear and trembling, and sometimes a shaky voice, near to tears. I was overwhelmed at the impact it had. Many hearers found it helpful. Individuals found it meaningful in different ways.

One kind of comment really touched me the most. Those were from widows or widowers who said, "Thanks so much for expressing it like it really is. I could never find the words or have the courage to speak them, but they need to be heard. Thanks for saying them for me."

Such affirmation somehow gave a sense of purpose to the learning I was receiving through my grief.

There were many fears to unearth and face after the death of my spouse—the fear of living alone, the fear of making decisions without a soulmate with whom to discuss it, the fear of handling my finances and more. However, in facing those and sharing them openly, I became able to encourage others to examine the roots of their fears and find release as they confronted their own. My encounter with death has most certainly enlarged my understanding of others who are going through the same kind of life happenings.

I found I didn't have to wait until I felt strong again to be able to share and help others. These verses encouraged me:

So take a new grip with your tired hands stand firm on your shaky legs, and mark out a straight path for your feet, so that those who follow you, though weak and lame, will not fall and hurt themselves but become strong. ... Look after each other so that not one of you will fail to find God's best blessings. [22]

A word fitly spoken is like apples of gold in settings of silver. [23]

A word fitly written has the same effect. I've personally experienced how a short note or a heartening word can pack a lot of encouraging power, especially if it's unexpected. The few cards I received on the anniversary of Norman's death were such a balm to me. I try to remember others the same way just by entering their name on my calendar for a year after the death of their loved one.

With Paul's death, I was able to more easily move into acceptance and then ministering to others, because many of my fears had already been faced. Without needing to work through those basic anxieties, my heart was more open to receive the sympathy and encouragement from others. I know now that to practise the ministry of understanding and encouragement, words don't need to be polished or

---

[22] Hebrews 12:12-13,15 (TLB)

[23] Proverbs 25:11 (RSV)

flowery—only sincere. They can be conveyed in something as simple as a postcard or sticky note, baked into cookies or casseroles, or delivered with a single flower from the garden. They can be conveyed over a cup of coffee, with a listening ear, a pat on the shoulder or a hug. I have been both receiver and giver of such.

Words and speaking are the avenue by which I am most apt to feel healing. For others, it may be something else. My willingness to be used allows God to show the path for me. I did discover ways to "not waste a good difficulty, but grow by it."

A Bitter Lesson

Alan Anderson

Part of my role as a spiritual care professional in a healthcare facility is to meet with people who are dying. They are my teachers. I approach each person with his or her own uniqueness in mind.

One morning the head nurse of the healthcare facility I worked in asked me to visit a patient after her doctor informed her she had a terminal illness. This lady became one of my teachers, although a reluctant one.

I knocked on the woman's door and said, "Hi, it's Alan, may I come in?"

When she agreed, I went into her room and sat with her. Thankfully, I had talked to her on numerous occasions previously. Perhaps knowing me helped her feel more at ease as we talked.

How are you feeling right now? I asked.

"I'm not sure."

She was sitting in her wheelchair by a window. I noticed how sad she looked.

"The nurse told me about the news of your illness." I came closer to her and sat in a chair.

"Yes, that's what I'm not sure of." She then clarified what she meant. "I'm not sure how I feel about it. I mean, he said I'm going to die!" She briefly looked at me then turned to look out the window.

"It must be a lot for you to process," I replied.

"Yes, I need some time to think about it. Maybe we can talk later." She turned her head and looked out the window.

"If that's what you want, then I can come back another time."

It seemed to me she was being emotionally guarded by not saying too much. I left her room to carry on with my day.

As I walked away from her room, the woman's need to think about her situation remained in my mind. It left me feeling sad, and that sadness is a mixed emotion. I felt sad for her trying to process the news she has been given about dying. I also felt sad that the moments in end of life situations are fleeting. I kept thinking perhaps I allowed the visit to end too soon.

I recorded brief notes from my visit in the woman's chart to show nursing staff that I followed up. This is standard procedure in healthcare. I then carried on with my day.

The next day a staff member informed me the patient had suffered a stroke during the night. She could no longer speak, as a result.

She wasn't conscious when I visited with her. I sat by her bed and said, "Hello, it's Alan. I know you can't talk. If it's okay, I will sit with you for a bit." She didn't respond, but I spoke to her with the hope she could hear me. I believe that sitting by the bed of a dying person is a sacred honour. My presence was all I could bring in such a vulnerable situation. I realized that she might never talk to anyone again.

I left the woman's room and the nurse approached me once again. She asked me to meet in the nursing station office for a few minutes to discuss the patient's situation. The busyness of healthcare often means professional caregivers put aside their emotions, including their grief, to concentrate on caring for patients. In my work as a spiritual care professional, I had opportunity to at least be available for staff when needed. This was one of these times.

Once the office door was closed, the nurse said, "Some people's situations get to me more than others. This woman's daughters are angry at their brother." She filled me in on some details to help me become more familiar with the patient's situation. "I'm more concerned about what you are feeling right now," I said.

"I never understand why some families can't put their differences aside at times like this. Their mother is dying and it doesn't seem to make a difference!" She looked frustrated as well as sad.

To affirm her feelings, I said, "You see a lot of sad situations in your work. It sounds like things build up inside you. You grieve for your patients."

"Yes, I do. I try to be professional, but now and then my emotions catch up with me," she stood and walked over to a file cabinet to pick out a file. It was as if she was trying to distract herself from her emotions.

"It is emotionally healthy for us to honour and name our feelings in our work," I smiled at her and stood up, ready to leave her office.

She concluded our time together by saying, "Thanks for listening to me, Alan. I thought spiritual care is only for patients or their family members."

I shook my head. "I'm here for staff as well. You have emotional and spiritual needs too," I assured her.

In the afternoon, I went to the patient's room again. When I know a patient is dying and family members might be present, I drop in frequently. The lady was still unconscious and unresponsive to voice or touch. She looked thinner to me as if she was wasting away before my eyes.

While I was sitting by her bedside, her two daughters entered the room. I met them during a previous visit and recognized them from the family photo on the lady's side table. They were both obviously having a tough time. It appeared as though they'd been crying.

Although it was sunny outside, one of the daughters

walked across the room and drew the curtains. This blocked out the sunlight and made the room seem darker and sadder.

The daughters offered me a quick hello, then turned their attention to their mother. They were upset and walked over to their mother's bed. For a minute or two, they stared at her and said nothing.

I stood and asked the daughters, "How are you doing right now?"

One of them began to cry. The other answered, "I can't believe the doctor told her she is dying. Who wants to be told that?"

"Yes, that is difficult and sad news to hear," I said.

The daughter who'd been crying said, "She can't die now. She has to wait."

"What does your mother have to wait for?" I was puzzled at her statement.

She began to cry again. Her sister said, "We have to call our brother. Mom has to wait for him."

I realized I was a witness to a family experiencing something new and unfamiliar to them. Their mother was dying. The daughters were distressed and sad, and they needed to call their brother and give him the news.

I remembered talking to the nurse and hearing her grief related to the matter. The scene thus far caused me to feel my own sense of sorrow. My empathetic presence in supporting the daughters meant that my sorrow, however, was not my focus. I was there to offer support to the ladies as they processed their thoughts and feelings in the moment.

The oldest daughter excused herself from the room to call her brother. Upon returning about a half hour later, it was obvious things did not go well with the phone call. She said she didn't want to talk in front of her mother, and so we went into the hallway to discuss the call.

"I am so mad at him right now!" She said, "I told him about mom and asked him to fly down and see her. I said he should come right away if he wants to see her before she dies." She added, "He said he can't come at all because he is busy."

At this point the younger sister began to cry again and muttered, "I don't want to talk about him. I'm going to sit with mom. At least we aren't deserting her!"

The older sister informed me that the head nurse knew the situation. She said the nurse would fill me in on details about the relationship between her brother and their mother.

She then said, "I'm going to sit with mom. Maybe I will talk to you later." With that she walked into her mother's room and closed the door.

I felt quite dismissed at the older sister's final words to me. I realized, however, that the family was experiencing a lot of grief. People can indeed seem dismissive and blunt due to their grief, but I did not take her remarks personally. On the other hand, I also experienced grief because of the family's sadness.

A few minutes later, I saw the nurse in her office and decided to discuss the patient's family situation with her. I informed her that one of the patient's daughters suggested I talk to her.

She said, "Yes, Alan, the daughters are really upset at their brother."

I asked her to elaborate for me so I could have a better understanding of their situation.

"A number of years ago, the mother and her son had a falling out," the nurse said. "The daughters said that she was not an easy person to live with. As they were growing up, their brother began to rebel against his mother's demands.

Something happened that distanced them from each

other. They have been apart for years. The girls are involved in their mother's life, but the brother really isn't."

"The reason the daughters are upset at their brother seems to go deeper than I thought." I pondered the situation.

The nurse went on, "Yes, it is all so very sad. Her son may not come and see his mom. As a matter of fact, I don't remember her even talking about him, at least to me. Maybe he thinks that now she can no longer talk, there is no point in coming to see her. Maybe to him, his business is first."

I wasn't really sure what to say other than, "I agree with you. It's very sad. Grief can be complex, perhaps especially in a situation like this."

As the nurse and I were ending our discussion, we heard a knock on the office door. The younger sister came in and asked to speak with us. She began to fill in some details about her thoughts on their family relationship.

She said, "My sister told me you're probably going to discuss things to do with our family. I just want to say, I don't think my brother will come to see mom. They have been separated for years. For some reason, she treated him differently than us. She isn't the most warm and caring person to have as a mother. She never made a point of telling us that she loved us. She didn't even make the effort to go to my brother's wedding. She has only seen his children one time. When he moved out on his own, I think that meant he finished with mom. Now it's too late. It didn't help that we nagged at him over the years."

The nurse informed me the next morning that the patient had died. Her daughters were loyal to the end and were sitting by her bed when she passed away. Perhaps by this act of love, they were still trying to please her. I was also told that the older sister phoned her brother one last time to come and see their mother. When she called him, he was ready to board a plane. He never saw his mother again. I wondered to myself what the son might have been thinking as he boarded the plane knowing his mother had died.

As I reflect on this situation, I see all the lessons from my teachers are tender or precious. I have never forgotten this bitter lesson. This mother seemingly deprived her children of hearing that she loved them. Family reconciliation sometimes falls short, even during a time of grief.

Perhaps in this lesson, hope can still be found. I still have time to continually nurture a healthy emotional relationship with my family. This includes letting them know I love them.

It means being a real part of their lives as much as possible. When my final breath comes, I know I will not be alone. I think most people want to know that they are loved. I know I do!

Remembering Alyssa

Carolyn Wilker

One Sunday morning in April, 2004, my parents received a telephone call. A cousin in northern Ontario had called to give them the sad news that his niece, Alyssa, had died. Mom relayed the news to my sisters and me.

Alyssa had gone bike riding with her brother who was just a few years older. They were travelling along the road when a car came along and hit Alyssa's bike, throwing her to the ground. She died soon after. All because of a drunk driver.

We hadn't had the pleasure of meeting Alyssa but we knew her father and his brother and sister, and her grandparents, well. Our family had spent hours together at their home and ours before they moved north. Now they reached out, asking for our prayers and moral support at this sad and difficult time.

We were more than a day's drive by car and none of us could be there with them on such short notice. We wrote cards, sent flowers, and donated to a special fund in memory of Alyssa. Nothing could take away the torment of this little girl's death. We ached for them all and we prayed, too, for her brother who had been there with her. We could do little else except weep.

I wished I had been closer geographically to comfort our cousins and their family with our hugs. All we could do was pray.

I asked my cousin Dennis, Alyssa's uncle, if he could tell us of their experience. He told me that the experience "sat heavily on him" until he could respond. Then he poured out his story:

My family and I were just sitting down to a group anniversary supper at the restaurant when we got the news about my seven-year-old niece, Alyssa.

We received a call to tell us she was in an accident and were asked to meet at the hospital as she wasn't going to make it. I felt shocked, in disbelief, and sick to my stomach. We all did. We had to go straight to the hospital emergency department and arrived there just after the ambulance. We were shaken to the core with loss and disbelief that she was gone.

In the small-town emergency department, we had access to the care room along with police, doctors, paramedics and nurses.

Everyone rushed to attend to Alyssa amid much chaos and confusion. We soon learned that Alyssa's head injuries were severe. She died quickly despite several attempts to revive her.

Alyssa's sudden death was at first traumatizing for us and our children, and then disbelief set in, but our children seemed to accept it sooner and move on a little more easily than the adults.

Our eldest son had a harder time and we talked about it on several occasions. Training as a paramedic, he would have to deal with such incidents as a regular occurrence. I said that everyone here was a 'professional' and they all had done the best they could—all that was physically possible to try to save Alyssa. The rest was in God's hands. I believed, even if it was difficult, that everything happened for a reason. Alyssa's death hit everyone so hard that promoting conversation with other paramedics and the police seemed to help everyone. I thanked each one individually for their assistance.

By supporting each other, we were able to work through the initial shock of what had happened. Tears flowed. Hugs comforted.

No one really knew what to say; often people just offered spiritual support. Sometimes just a touch, a smile or tear helped. In the days that followed, there were times when we wanted to be alone.

It was a terrible feeling accompanied with the sense that we needed someone to "pull us out of it." It was like a bad dream. The local community helped us through the first days and week with one-on-one conversations and many visits.

They brought food and offered emotional support. Our whole family welcomed the support. Without it despair was inevitable, so we appreciated the touch of close family, friends, and neighbours bringing food. We didn't want to cook, or cater to visitors, so the dishes were set out for self-serve as we wished to eat. The gesture and companionship it brought was consoling.

We all felt helpless and swept into funeral arrangements and all that goes with it, without time to think or properly grieve. Alyssa's parents really struggled with the death of their daughter. The rest of the family carried on as best we could.

I wrote a poem—"Why Alyssa?"—expressing my thoughts about our physical loss, and the pain that went with it. It helped.

With so many people involved in community activities in the small towns near our home, they soon learned the story, from people in business, to sports and academic people.

The crowded church for Alyssa's funeral spoke of a supportive community. When there was no more room in the church, local people spilled out into the streets and parking lots. There were people everywhere—buses filled with school children, members of police, fire crew, teachers and nurses. All of them had compassion for us and the needless loss to the family and community because of a drunk driver accident.

My poem, "Why Alyssa?" was read during the service, and later it was published in the newspaper.

Sometime after the funeral, people from the organization Mothers Against Drunk Driving became involved, and with local volunteers, they set up an annual bicycle rodeo in Alyssa's name. Police, firemen and other people taught bicycle safety. We were encouraged by this action.

I think a strong faith in God played a big part for my family and me in our healing. Even though it wasn't easy, I know that moving forward and realizing life had to go on had to be my focus. With Alyssa's parents, I think they lost too much faith and couldn't move forward.

When you're stuck in the past with such great hurt, how do you move forward? For some, perhaps acceptance is too big of a challenge. Maybe prayer is the best hope for their future.

We've kept a picture of Alyssa on a dresser with a copy of my poem. I've given a copy to anyone who asked. I believe that Alyssa is still with us and guides and protects all who ask. I think of this quote by Ann Landers, "Some people believe holding on and hanging in there are signs of great strength. However, there are times when it takes much more strength to know when to let go and to do it!" This could be true in grief as well.

I've always been sensitive to funerals, death and dying, and only in the last years have accepted it as a more natural process (in most cases). I view a funeral as a celebration of life here and beyond, which is more comforting and helps shift our inherent fear of the unknown into faith. Something I do that helps me in grief is writing a daily journal and collecting quotes, and the words of this one by Ann Landers comes to mind today as I write.

Many years later it's still difficult for Dennis and his family to revisit what happened, much less write about it. Alyssa's life was important to celebrate and to remember.

I've learned that the best thing I can do for someone who is grieving is to be a good listener. If I pay attention and let those who are grieving share as I would like to be heard if it were me, then my empathy is real.

Having compassion and praying for parents whose child has died can be an encouragement for them to one day talk about their great loss and perhaps find a way to move forward.

Though Alyssa would be a young adult at the time of this writing, we know that the hurt lasts a long time. Alyssa may not be a part of every conversation we have with our northern cousins, but she's part of their life and our history together.

If a Doorbell Could Take Messages[24]

Carolyn Wilker

It would tell that I've been there
rooted to the doorstep

If a doorbell had feelings
it would read
constricted throat
listening for footsteps

Today
your cat answers
stretching himself against the screen
wanting out

does he miss you like I do?

If a doorbell could record my presence
the warmth of the cement on which I stand
the moment diverted from my tangled path
you'd know that I think of you

---

[24] Published by Tower Poetry, Winter edition, 2007-2008, Volume 56, No. 2

Pressing 9

Glynis M Belec

"I've got some bad news."

A sick feeling rises in my throat every time I listen to the voice mail message from my brother.

"Sue's dead."

Over and over, it's like a stabbing knife in my chest. Two years have passed and I still cannot bring myself to erase John's crushing words from my telephone.

"Press seven to delete your message. Press nine to save."

Every time, I press 9.

When I listen to John's heartbreaking, tear-filled words, I am still in the moment. I cry all over again with John's recorded message and think of how riddled with guilt he was at first for not finding our sister, Sue, earlier. Especially since he rented the basement apartment in her home.

I, too, felt guilty because I should have called her more often. I knew she had been having health issues and many times I did try.

But Sue was a fiercely independent free spirit. If she didn't want to answer the phone, she jolly well wouldn't. If she wanted to lock her door and not let anyone in, she certainly would do that.

Sue didn't want to hear me talk about prayer or God or hope. She had her own set of beliefs and valued her privacy. It wasn't unusual for her to tell John that she would be staying in her room and not to bother her. John needed not to feel guilty. But we all did.

Sue had always been that way. Even as a child she was bold and rebellious. If someone told her "no", she would hear "yes" and was wont to explore beyond any so-called limitations. Her daring attitude opened a lot of wonderful doors, but it also got her into a lot of trouble.

For years Sue battled many health issues. Lupus. Fibromyalgia. Chronic Obstructive Pulmonary Disease. Depression. It seemed her time had come. No more was Sue able to 'call the shots.'

As I drove the two hours to Sue's home, all I could think of were her two daughters. Angie, her eldest, a counsellor—who would offer her the counsel she would need? And Jenny, Sue's youngest—my heart hurt for her. She was the one I spoke to when I called back after I got John's message. Her trembling voice was like a little girl lost. I wanted to reach down the phone line, rub her back like I did when she was a baby and tell her it would be okay.

But it wasn't okay. I arrived at Sue's place exactly the same time as Angie. A plain cube van was parked outside the house. Jenny and John stood on the porch, crying. Angie and I embraced and then panic set in. A man was just closing the back of the van.

"Stop!" I think Angie and I said, simultaneously. "We want to see her."

The coroner told us he would unzip the shroud but we had to be quick, and under no circumstance could we touch Sue. A person who has been declared dead for 24 hours requires a different protocol.

Angie, who usually has the same fortitude as my beautiful sister, crumpled when she saw her mother's lifeless body. I wanted to lean over and stroke my little sister's face and call her back. I wanted to 'pull a Sue' and hear yes instead of no. Go ahead and deal with the consequences later. But I knew I couldn't touch my sister even for one last time. Instead I felt the vomit rise and the sorrow cut deep. My feet felt like cement blocks. Convulsive tears consumed any desire I might have had to stay strong for my nieces. I wanted to crawl in the back of the van with Sue and will her back to life.

The attendant asked Angie and me to step away from the van. We obeyed begrudgingly. The door closed.

It was the last time we would see her. My little sister was gone. Forever.

Fast forward two years. My head becomes clearer but the same heaviness in my heart remains for my little sister, especially when I see the photos of us as children.

"Rosemary, Glynis, Susan and John. Acts and Apostles follow on," Mom used to say. Perfect rhythm. Four beats. One big sister. One little sister. One little brother. We balanced each other out, but now the balance is off kilter. Our rhythm has gone awry.

Angie and Jenny are not aware that I still have the message on my phone. One day I will tell them. I think they might smile and understand why I don't want to erase that moment, no matter how horrible it was. Or maybe 'counsellor' Angie will tell me I should only press 7 when I am ready.

I want to know how Angie and Jenny are doing. We don't see each other much, but thank goodness for social media. Once in a while, we touch base.

Next time we chat, I ask the girls what it was like for them. I haven't asked them before. I was too wrapped up in my own grief.

"It was like time stood still," Angie says, thinking about that day. "I was at a conference and stepped out to take the call. I just stood there when someone from the conference asked if all was ok. I simply said, 'I think I have to go. My mom is dead.'"

Jenny doesn't fumble for words. "I remember every

detail. I had been trying to call Mom and she never answered," which Jenny knew was not unusual.

Then when Jenny's phone rang, she was happy to see it was her mother's number showing up on the call display. But it was a firefighter who gave her the terrible news and then he handed the phone over to John. Jenny could barely process it.

"I heard John on the line sobbing that he was sorry, over and over again. I've never heard John cry like that and I hope I never do again. I tried asking what happened, but I couldn't make out what he was saying, so I told him I would be right there."

Both Angie and Jenny desperately made arrangements. Sue had taught both girls how to take control. They didn't have it easy over the years, but both girls emerged as strong women. The fruit of Sue's labour was showing. Angie and Jenny, although heartbroken, devastated and crushed, stepped up to the plate and worked together in their initial grief.

"From the day I found out to now, I think I've run the gamut with emotions," Jenny says, as she contemplates her mom's massive heart attack and seemingly untimely death.

"I have good days and bad days, and really horrible days." Jenny deals with it by focusing on her own family and their future. "I don't hold back my tears when I'm alone. I think crying helps get out the bad thoughts. I talk about Mom and to her sometimes."

Angie admits to feeling lost even now. "It's like you lose your footing—your grounding anchor. I truly became an orphan that day."

She admits that her faith in the afterlife and her personal belief system has helped.

"I feel Mom's presence often."

Jenny thinks about the time right after her mom's death when she went into the bush behind her house.

"I screamed and cried and yelled."

She says when she thinks of her mother, now, it's more a mixture of sadness and happiness.

"I'm not angry anymore. I think letting it all out helped me immensely."

Both girls agree that their grieving never stops, though.

"There will always be moments that I need, miss, want, my mommy. Those moments will always be accompanied by grief," Jenny says, wiping away a tear.

Angie likens her grief to a backpack that she cannot remove. It has become part of her. She wants people to talk to her about her grief and her mother. Because she has counselling experience, Angie knows the importance of talking about trauma and trials.

"From the beginning, I have encouraged people to talk about Mom, because she did exist and she existed well. People stop talking about her when they see me tear up."

Angie doesn't want people to stop talking about her mother.

"Sometimes I will talk to her. Sometimes I'll put on a song she liked. Sometimes I'll have a whiskey in her honour."

Angie has been educated in how to care for and counsel others, but sometimes she finds it hard to listen to herself.

She continues to try and although she hasn't had grief counselling, she keeps herself busy and practises good self-care. It's also important to Angie to tell her children how proud Grandma was of them.

Jenny also chose not to have grief counselling. Like her mother, she describes herself as a private person who would have great difficulty sharing her heart with a complete stranger.

"I have a wonderful family and great friends who are always ready with an ear to listen," Jenny says. And she copes by living her life day to day, one step at a time, and appreciating the strong woman she has become, because of the influence of her mother.

Jenny believes death is a spiritual experience. "I believe that Mom was needed somewhere else. I just feel like her soul was done with this life and she's on to the next adventure."

When I listen now to my two beautiful nieces as they talk about their mother, I am touched by their closeness and the way they support each other. Sue really did do a good job of teaching both girls about the importance of family. I feel sad they have lost their mother, but I am proud of the way they don't see their grief as a weakness, but rather as a part of their lives.

Someday I will press 7, but for now I will plod on with my memories of Sue. I will remember the good times and Sue's unconditional love. She might have been tough on the outside, but she had a kind and generous heart that touched so many—including me, her sad, big sister.

The Kitchen Table

Glynis M Belec

Matt's father, Jim, lost his battle to Amyotrophic Lateral Sclerosis (ALS) within a year of diagnosis. I spoke with Matt a few months after his father's death because I wanted to know how he was doing and how he was grieving. I wanted to find out if being a first responder made a difference in the way one grieves.

Matt has a unique perspective because of his job. He's a firefighter. Facing death is part of his everyday life. But what about when it's a family member? Does that make a difference? I was about to find out. I asked Matt what got him through each day after his father's death.

I work as a firefighter in a large city, and our job exposes us to injury, illness, and death, daily. As unfortunate as that may be, I feel that it softened the blow of Dad being diagnosed [with ALS] and rapidly losing his health. I can't exactly specify what my coping mechanisms are for what I experience at work, but whatever they are, they have allowed me to process everything about Dad's death a bit differently. I would hate to think that I've grown cold and numb to tragedy, but there definitely is an element of that involved as I try to cope.

There's a magical place in every firehouse. It's called The Kitchen Table. It's a one-stop-shop and includes a therapist, doctor, counsellor, contractor, pastor, politician, financial advisor, tech wiz, chef, mechanic, travel agent, and every other problem-solving position imaginable.

What may seem like a big problem, or unfathomable

mystery in the morning, seems to disappear after grabbing a cup of coffee and a seat at that table. There are few secrets around The Kitchen Table, and a good dose of humility is a pre-requisite for admittance. By default, I feel like a lot of my coping happens around this table, simply due to the amount of time spent at the firehouse.

As much as it's a place where we poke fun at each other at any given opportunity, it's also a place where everyone brings their joys and burdens, marriage struggles, problems with kids, pregnancy announcements, politics and more. It's where I broke the news to my guys when Dad was diagnosed with that wretched disease. I remember thinking I could keep it together that morning. I should have known better. But I was glad I was there.

When one of us is down, the rest step it up, support each other, and when the alarms go off, we get on the truck and go.

It's this 'getting back on the horse' mentality that Dad always had. Bad things happen— we can choose to stew over them, or accept them and move forward. This has allowed me to get on with my days relatively smoothly since Dad died.

That being said, I'm not always at The Kitchen Table. I have my private moments where everything seems to come to a grinding halt, even if just for a few seconds.

I struggle to find an easy description for how these moments feel. It's an uneasiness in my chest, an absent breath, a vacuum that pulls all emotion away for mere seconds, and a reminder that Dad's gone. Sometimes it's an old picture or video that I come across on social media, seeing or smelling something that reminds me of an activity we did together, or even when I catch myself having a 'Dad' moment with my own kids. I remember sharing similar times with Dad.

And then as a Christian, I find myself seated at another kind of table, the one with an open Bible. I have to trust God's Word. I need to hold firm knowing He has our best interests in mind, and He will see me and my family through. If we believe there is something beyond our time here on Earth, then we should have no fear of death. We read about it in scripture. We listen to sermons preached on eternal life. We sing about it, and it forms the foundation of evangelical ministry—eternal Salvation in a perfect and joy-filled place.

If I truly believe, I shouldn't find it hard understanding Dad's time here was finished, and he has now passed into eternity. That's my comfort.

It hurt to see Dad suffer. It hurt to remember what he went through during his final weeks and months. Now I seek the good.

I've discovered the good is found in reminding myself that whatever brings us happiness in this life, it pales in comparison to what God has promised us.

We often think of heaven as some place up in the clouds, or some monstrous city made of gold, with pearly gates, and angels flying around, playing harps all day. Sounds pretty boring to me!

I don't profess to be an expert on the scriptures, but I know God's Word speaks of a New Heaven and a New Earth—a redeemed Earth that has been returned to its former glory, one that is very good. I believe that this is what heaven will be like. God has blessed us with skills and abilities. Using them gives us satisfaction and joy. I believe we will use these same capabilities to care for God's Kingdom—as He originally intended—for our eternal joy. And more importantly, we will enjoy companionship with other believers, family included.

When I'm away from The Kitchen Table and experience

moments of grief, I quickly turn my thoughts to what Dad is likely doing in heaven. Fishing, hunting, loving his neighbours, and caring for God's kingdom.

I miss being able to share experiences and dreams with my Dad. I miss walking through a field on a crisp November morning, waiting for a deer to make its way out of the forest. I long for the insurmountable peace that can only be found standing on a boat in a quiet bay, in search of the biggest fish on the lake.

I miss building things with my dad, and enjoying a cold rye and coke at the end of the day. I still hear the rhythm of his finger snapping, his whistling, and his various mannerisms that I catch myself doing more and more every day. I miss the joy on his face whenever we would go home to visit, especially with his grandkids in tow. I recall the look on his face when he couldn't catch a break during a hand of playing cards. I will always remember how much love he had for Mom, for our family, and for his community. All of these things I miss, but more importantly, I will never forget.

For me, grief over Dad, over lost friends, over people I've stood beside and sat with as they passed away, despite my best efforts as a first responder, has made me increasingly more aware of how fleeting life can be, and how in the blink of an eye, everything can change. It has made me more grateful for what we have, and for the joy and wonder that surrounds us, yet often goes unnoticed.

Each person deals with grief differently, and with different timelines. I believe grief eventually loses its sting, and transitions from feelings of deep heart-wrenching sadness to fond memories and joyful recollection—good grief, so to speak.

There's a saying in the fire service, and I've heard it more than once at The Kitchen Table: "I wish my mind could forget what my eyes have seen." I find this a fitting phrase when it comes to grieving. I don't think grief ever goes away. It gets easier, it becomes a new normal, but it doesn't disappear.

Dad's gone. A piece of my heart went with him. But I can hear him now—he's sitting at a kitchen table, cheering us all on.

Afterword

Lisa Elliot

Good grief. Is there such a thing? I think so. Let me rephrase that. I know so. How? I've experienced it in a personal and profound way. I have faced, and painstakingly embraced, every parent's worst nightmare.

At eighteen years of age, my son Ben was the second oldest of our four children. He was at the peak of life, healthy, strong, athletic, and eagerly preparing to attend university in order to embark on a promising future. When my husband called me from the local hospital to inform me that Ben had collapsed at the restaurant where he was working and was now undergoing a bone marrow aspirate, it didn't make any sense. Within the next twenty-four hours, Ben was diagnosed with acute lymphoblastic leukemia. With this uninvited intruder barging into my home, my family determinedly chose to live fully in every moment we had amid the reality of Ben's impending death. We hoped for the best while we prepared for the worst. And the worst did come. Ben was promoted to his heavenly home one-year-and-one-week after his diagnosis.

Strangely, as the seed of the worst kind was planted in my heart, the best slowly took root while God tenderly nurtured the soil of my heart and breathed life back into the dry dust. I am, indeed, a living testament that there is life beyond the grave. I can tell you firsthand that grief is good. Through the process of grief, God has touched and healed the otherwise impenetrable recesses of my heart that no human hand can touch. You see, I am a good grief person, much like the contributors of this book.

Death can be ugly and harsh. Be it a spouse, a sibling, a close friend, a parent, a grandparent, an unborn child or one that is years, months, or minutes old—you've read about it over and over again from those who have willingly and vulnerably shared their stories in *Good Grief People*.

Anyone who has ventured down the unknown and unpredictable road of grief can attest to the fact that once you've experienced significant loss and death you will never be the same. However, when it is embraced rather than shunned, confronted rather than avoided, processed rather than stifled—when the bereft can be honest about it, work with it, and grow through it to reap valuable lessons from it and, in turn, use it to reach into the lives of others—that, my friend, is good grief!

Perhaps you're among those who are not only asking how any grief can be good, but how a God who claims to be good can allow suffering, pain, and loss. Good question. We've probably all asked it at one time or another. In fact, there are many questions that invade and consume our hearts and minds. The good news is that our good God grants us permission to ask these questions. In fact, He invites us to ask them.

Jesus even asked the question that haunts each of us when faced with an untimely and significant loss, "Why?" as He hung on the cross, mocked, beaten, betrayed, and abandoned. The Bible tells us that Jesus was a man of sorrows, acquainted with grief.[25] Jesus wept at the gravesite of one of His closest friends.[26] God records and collects every tear we cry.[27]

---

[25] Isaiah 53

[26] John 11:35

[27] Psalm 55:8

I can't speak for others, but when I get to heaven I immediately plan to dive heart-first into a salt-water pool filled with my own tears. After all, there is healing in salt. Although He may not answer our questions this side of heaven, He can handle them. After all, He watched His own Son suffer and die. My Ben would say, "He just gets it, folks!"

I believe that grief is a gift from the Giver of Life who has the power over death. Scripture tells us that the LORD is close to the broken-hearted and saves those who are crushed in spirit.[28] When we draw close to Him, He will draw close to us.[29] He hears our cry and pulls us out of the miry pit.[30] He walks with us through the valley of the shadow of death. His rod and staff comfort us. He leads us beside still water and restores our souls.[31]

The problem is ultimately not in whether the experience of grief is good or bad. Rather, it's that we don't allow ourselves to fully embrace or engage in it. As human beings, and even as believers in the Lord, Jesus Christ, we are far too quick to try to alleviate not only our own pain but also the pain of others. We use flippant remarks like, "Things will look better in the morning" and "It'll all work out, you'll see." People want to offer a simple remedy or quick-fix—if it were only that easy.

Even in Christian circles Bible verses, like where it says that all things work together for good,[32] for instance, are carelessly slapped onto gaping wounds, most likely in a meagre effort to overcome the would-be comforters own helpless attempt to ease the pain.

---

[28] Psalm 34:18

[29] James 4:8

[30] Psalm 40:1-4

[31] Psalm 23

[32] Romans 8:28—a paraphrase

It's been communicated throughout *Good Grief People* that there is undeniable good that comes out of our grief when we allow it to do its intended transforming work.

The ultimate hope is that one day there will be no more death at the great appearance of our Lord, Jesus. He is going to meet us at heaven's gate and wipe every tear from our eyes.

There will be no more death or mourning or crying or pain, for the old order of things has passed away.[33] On that wonderful day, our questions won't matter anymore. We'll stand back in awe as God reveals HIS-story. One by one the pages of our lives will be turned and finally help us make sense of them in their proper context.

All of us have grief in common. It's where we all meet at the foot of the cross. Death is as much a reality as life. And through the process of grief, we are given the opportunity to taste and see that the Lord is good.[34] In my own experience, that's what makes grief so good, people!

Each person's story in this book has been shared from a personal heart-treasury. Although each grief experience is personal and unique, it is my hope and prayer that those of you who have lost loved ones are comforted. And that those who have not yet experienced grief are better prepared.

Lisa

[33] Revelation 21:4

[34] Psalm 34:8

Getting Through

This might be a place for you to find a few words of solace, comfort and focus. Sometimes when we grieve, being contemplative helps. We have presented a few quotes and bits of advice here for those who grieve and for those who want to help others during their sorrow.

"Those who are dying know it. Many of them may teach me about the beauty and wonder of silence. Silence is also a teacher if I but listen. I am learning to slow things down. To escape the unnecessary clamour. The noise, all too close. If I listen I will learn how present silence is.

Alan

"It is your grief. It can't be totally understood by anyone else. However, what can be understood by others, is your need for unconditional love, and support. Be blessed knowing others do care, even if they don't understand. And when it comes down to it, we are all just walking each other home."

Alan

"Losing everything is like the sun going down on me."

Elton John, Musician

"Being broken isn't the worst thing. We can be mended and put together again. We don't have to be ashamed of our past. We can embrace the history that gives us value, and see our cracks as beautiful."

Anna White, Author

"I know now that we never get over great losses; we absorb them, and they carve us into different, often kinder, creatures."

Gail Caldwell, Author

". . . after someone you love dies, the most daunting task you face is rebuilding your life and finding a new identity."

Susan Berger, Author

"The grief I've known in life will never be healed. No one can take it back. You have to learn to pack up your scars and keep going, headed for the future. If I spend time licking my wounds, I'm not moving forward."

Jose Musico, Uraguay's former President

"Count it all joy, my brethren, when you meet various trials, for you know that the testing of your faith produces steadfastness. And let steadfastness have its full effect, that you may be perfect and complete, lacking in nothing."

James 1:2-4

After Tom died at the hospice, he was laid on a stretcher, his face showing, and a beautiful hand-made cloth was draped over the rest of his body.

We left his room in single file, and he was quietly wheeled down the hall in a simple processional led by a staff member carrying a burning candle.

At the waiting hearse, we said our last goodbyes. Tom's candle was placed in a beautiful sculpture setting near the exit where it would burn for the next twenty-four hours.

How wonderful that his death was honoured in this way and not hidden away from everyone as something not to be seen. It was a true acknowledgement and acceptance of his death.

Barbara

"I do not at all understand the mystery of grace – only that it meets us where we are but does not leave us where it found us."

Anne Lamott, Author

"Once you learn how to die, you learn how to live."
Morrie from Mitch Albom's Tuesdays With Morrie

"Death ends a life, not a relationship."
Morrie from Mitch Albom's Tuesdays With Morrie

"Letting go of our suffering is the hardest work we will ever do. It is also the most fruitful. To heal means to meet ourselves in a new way – in the newness of each moment where all is possible and nothing is limited to the old."

Stephen Levine, Author

"Give sorrow words; the grief that does not speak knits up the o-er wrought heart and bids it break."

William Shakespeare, Macbeth

"Just when the caterpillar thought the world was over, it became a butterfly."

Anonymous

On Losing a Spouse

"The hardest thing about losing my husband didn't really kick in right away for me. I was too busy. It's when everything was done, all loose ends tied up, paperwork completed, the party was over and there was a kind of finality to it all.

Then the hard part began. For me it was trying to figure out where I fit in with Mike's family. I wasn't a blood relation. We had no children together. There were no deep emotional ties (it was a second marriage). I didn't know how hard I was supposed to try to stay in their lives or if I should just do the casual thing and see them when there is an invitation or when I run into them. The silence from them was deafening."

"I appreciated when people just said, 'I am so sorry, I can't imagine how you feel.'"

"I absolutely hated when someone would say to me, 'He's in a better place and out of pain' or 'give yourself time to heal. Things will get better.'"

"Staying in touch with me helps. A call or message on social media or a quick text."

"It didn't help when someone said, 'If there is anything I can do for you, let me know' but knowing they didn't mean it. I found most people don't mean it or at least don't follow up on it."

Kristina, a grieving widow

Good Things to Say and Do for Those Who Grieve

- ✓ Listen, listen, listen
- ✓ Say you don't know all they're going through, but you are trying to imagine what it would be like
- ✓ Ask what they liked best about their loved one
- ✓ Tell how you miss their loved one, too
- ✓ Tell what you liked about the loved one
- ✓ Take the person who is grieving out for a meal or ask him/her to your house for a visit
- ✓ Ask her to accompany you on a shopping trip, for an activity or a concert, movie or other activity
- ✓ If they are a widow/er take a meal or two that can be put in a freezer for later
- ✓ Find out important dates such as birthdays or anniversaries and send a note, an email or make a telephone call on those days
- ✓ Offer a hug
- ✓ Give a sincere compliment
- ✓ Let the bereaved know you are there to help if they need it. Make sure you mean it though and offer specific suggestions
- ✓ Shine everyone's shoes in the house for the funeral
- ✓ Bring a casserole over two weeks after the funeral
- ✓ Send a hand-written 'just thinking of you' card
- ✓ Clear the driveway of snow or mow the lawn
- ✓ Sit in silence and have a tissue handy
- ✓ Allow the person to cry
- ✓ Offer to pray
- ✓ Ask how they are coping
- ✓ We all need help at times like this, I am here for you

What NOT to Say to Those Who Grieve

- × "I know JUST how you feel." Your relationship and circumstances will still be different even if you have lost a loved one
- × Never compare someone's death to how you felt losing a pet
- × "It will get better soon"
- × 'Time will heal.' Don't assume that six months – or any set period of time, is long enough for someone to grieve
- × Don't keep reminding the bereaved that the loved one is in a better place
- × Don't say things like, "You know you got to enjoy each other for many years and did a lot of wonderful things together." (Yes, we did, but I wanted more!)
- × "What stage of grief are you experiencing?"
- × "Other people have suffered losses too. You will be all right"
- × "She was not meant to suffer any longer" or "It was for the best"
- × "God needed a special angel"
- × "It was God's plan"
- × "It was meant to be this way"
- × "She did what she came here to do and it was her time to go"
- × "You just need to get back to your old self"
- × "Chin up. Life goes on"
- × "It will be all right"
- × "There is a reason for everything"
- × "You can still have another child. You're young enough"

Resources

Sudden Infant Death Syndrome - SIDS Network
Website: http://www.sids-network.org

Pregnancy and Infant Loss Network - PAIL
Website: http://pailnetwork.ca
PAIL Network is committed to making a positive difference to those affected by pregnancy and infant loss.

Online Support Group
http://www.babycenter.ca/c25001575/grief-and-loss-groups

Rainbows Canada
Website: http://www.rainbows.ca
Guiding Kids Through Life's Storms
An international organization experienced with grieving youth and adults.
Suite 545, 80 Bradford Street
Barrie, ON
L4N 6S7
Phone: 1-877-403-2733
Local: 705-726-7407
Fax: 705-726-5805
Email: admin@rainbows.ca

Bereaved Families of Ontario
Watline Postal Outlet P.O. Box 10015
Mississauga, Ontario
L4Z 4G5 info@bereavedfamilies.net
http://www.bereavedfamilies.net

You may also contact one of our affiliates directly:

REGION
- Cornwall and area www.bfocornwall.ca 613-936-1455
- Durham Region www.bfodurham.net 905-579-4293 1-800-387-4870
- Halton/Peel (Mississauga, Brampton and area) www.bereavedfamilies.ca 905-848-4337
- Hamilton/Burlington www.bfo-hamiltonburlington.on.ca 905-318-0070
- Kingston Region www.bfo-kingston.ca 613-634-1230 1-877-823-2601
- London-Southwest Region www.bfo.london.on.ca 519-686-1573
- Midwest (Kitchener/Waterloo, Cambridge, Guelph) www.bfomidwest.org 519-603-0196
- Ottawa Region www.bfo-ottawa.org 613-567-4278
- Pembroke www.griefsupport.ca 613-732-7894
- Peterborough 705-743-7233 1-866-887-2912
- Toronto www.bfotoronto.ca 416-440-0290
- York Region (Newmarket) www.bfoyr.com 905-898-6265 1-800-969-6904

WebHealing
General Information on Grief - Grief and Healing
Website: http://www.webhealing.com/
This site provides many resources on grief and healing.

Grief Net
Website: http://griefnet.org/
A collection of resources for those dealing with a loss. GriefNet.org is an Internet community of persons dealing

with grief, death, and major loss.

Death and Survivor Benefits

Website: http://www.hrsdc.gc.ca

Find information about the Death Benefit and Survivor Benefits for children, answers questions on how to apply, who is eligible etc.

Last Post Fund

For veterans

Website: http://www.lastpostfund.ca

Find out about the Last Post Fund, benefits, how to apply and who is eligible. Find contact information for the Last Post Fund as well as what services are available.

Willowgreen

http://www.willowgreen.com/

Willowgreen provides resources in the areas of illness, dying, grief and loss. Meaningful resources for hope, healing and inspiration.

The Virtual Hospice

Website: http://www.virtualhospice.ca

The Canadian Virtual Hospice provides support and personalized information about palliative and end-of-life care, loss and bereavement to patients, family members, health care providers, researchers and educators.

The Canadian Association for Suicide Prevention (CASP)

Coping Strategies for Living With Suicide Grief

Website: http://suicideprevention.ca/grieving/suicide-grief/

Grief and Bereavement
http://www.cancer.ca/en/cancer-information/cancer-journey/advanced-cancer/grief-bereavement/?region=on

The COPING Centre Head Office
http://www.copingcentre.com/
For detailed information concerning COPING worldwide
Contact: Glenn & Ros Crichton
1740 Blair Rd, Cambridge, ON N3H 4R8
Ph: 519-650-0852 or 1-877-554-4498
coping@copingcentre.com

Canadian Mental Health Association, National
http://www.cmha.ca/mental_health/grieving/#.WJE-kFMrLIV
info@cmha.ca
2301-180 Dundas Street West
Toronto, ON M5G 1Z8
613-745-7750

VON Sakura House
#715180 Oxford County Rd 4
Phone: (519) 537-8515
RR 5 Woodstock, ON
N4S 7V9
sakurahouse@von.ca
www.facebook.com/vonsakurahouse

Lisaard House
Email: admin@lisaardhouse.com
990 Speedsville Road, Cambridge, ON. N3H 4R6
Phone: 519-650-1121
Fax: 519-650-8058

Innisfree House
2375 Homer Watson Blvd.
Kitchener, ON
N2P 0E9
Phone: 519-208-5055
Fax: 519-208-5455

GriefShare
www.Griefshare.org
nancyguthrie.com

Hospice Wellington
Coordinating body for all grief support groups in Guelph.
Call for a referral.
795 Scottsdale Dr.
Guelph, ON N1G 3R8
Phone: 519-836-3921

Grief Recovery Institute
https://www.griefrecoverymethod.com/
Bereavement support for coping with death and loss as well
as certified grief counselor training courses.

References

1. Mann, Donna J. WinterGrief:. Belleville, Ont.: Essence Pub., 2003. Print.

2. Mann, Donna. Grieve and Grow: Practical Thoughts about Grief. Elora: Manna Publications, 2001. Print.

3. Mann, Donna. 21 Promises: Honouring Self in Grief. Elora: Kindle/Mann, 2015. Print. Kindle.

4. Mann, Donna. "Grieve and Grow." grieveandgrow.wordpress.com. Donna Mann.

5. Elliot, Lisa. "Grief in the Raw." *Just Between Us* Sept.-Oct. 2010

6. Fink, Constance. "Living Through Loss with Purpose." *Just Between Us* Spring 2013

7. Elliot, Lisa. "When the Holidays Hurt." *Just Between Us* Winter 2014

8. Elliot, Ben, September 14th 2009, Ten Days Before Dying, https://youtu.be/rK4P3axkhag. Stratford

9. DavidLisae, July 6, 2010, This is Life, https://www.youtube.com/watch?v=XyCt1f_ULkc

10. Choosing to Live through Loss with Purpose http://100huntley.com/watch?id=217121&title=choosing-to-live-through-loss-with-purpose

11. Dancing in the Rain: One Family's Journey Through Grief http://100huntley.com/watch?id=222425&title=dancing-in-the-rain-one-familys-journey-through-grief

Meet the Authors

Alan Anderson was born in Dundee, Scotland. His parents decided to emigrate in 1964 when Alan was ten years old. The family settled in British Columbia and Alan has lived there ever since.

Alan and his wife, Terry, have been married for 38 years. They have three children, six grandchildren and five grandchildren in heaven.

Alan loves to write about the deep things in life. He writes from a heart touched by grief and held by hope. A lot of his writings are about grief, suffering and hope and often his public speaking opportunities have been in the same vein.

The nature of Alan's writing stems from his almost 40 years of coming alongside people who are hurting as well as his personal experiences with grief.

God has gifted Alan with patience, presence and excellent listening skills. His caring attitude shines throughout his writing.

caledomiaspirit@gmail.com

Glynis M Belec also emigrated with her family from Scotland when she was ten years old. But she didn't know Alan at the time! She lives in Ontario with her husband, Gilles and they have been married for 38 years, too. She has two children plus one step son. Spending time with her wonderful grandchildren inspires her writing.

As an award-winning children's author and freelance writer Glynis thoroughly enjoys helping out other authors and especially beginning writers. She is constantly inspired by the world around her and the joy she finds in the simpler things in life.

Glynis is an inspirational speaker and one of her favourite topics to speak on is HOPE. She loves to find hope in the everyday even though sometimes it's hard, especially when a loved one dies. That has happened many times in her life but she continues to trust God and keep the faith.

www.glynisbelec.com

Barbara Heagy is a retired teacher and present day writer, photographer, traveller, and dancer. Her education reflects her eclectic interests; she has earned an honours BA with a major in Recreation, an honours Bachelor of Education, and a Master of Arts with a major in Dance.

Since the age of seventeen, Barbara has been filling empty journals and notebooks with her thoughts, musing and life experiences, while writing plays, poetry, essays, and stories that reflect life issues.

The loss of her beloved husband Tom, led her to publish

her personal inspirational memoir called *10 – A Story of Love, Life, and Loss*. Her story "Balm for the Spirit" about Tom's hospice experience is included in the book, *You Are Not Alone – 52 Stories of Hope*.

www.barbaraheagy.com

Donna Mann is married to Doug and she is a mother, grandmother and even has great-grands.

The death of a daughter took Donna into grief work: studying it through the eyes of sociology and scripture. She sees grief as one of life's gifts, not one you would request, but once received and put to work proves to be life-giving. She has written books, newspaper articles, emails and blogs offering both the psychological and experiential dimensions of grief.

One of Donna's favourite roles in ministry was spending time with families whose loved one was dying. It was a time to listen with the heart, comfort with words and yes, even make the coffee.

www.donnamann.org

Ruth Smith Meyer became quite familiar with grief through the death of Norman, her husband of 39 years, then after ten years of a second happy marriage, the death of Paul.

As an inspirational speaker, Ruth continues to resource

many diverse groups. She is the author of two adult novels— *Not Easily Broken* and *Not Far from the Tree,* a children's book—*Tyson's Sad Bad Day* and her memoirs—*Out of the Ordinary.* She has also been included in several anthologies.

Ruth enjoys her wonderful families—the four children to whom she gave birth and four blessings from her second marriage. To these have been added, spouses, a total of eighteen grandchildren and six great-grands.

www.ruthsmithmeyer.com

Carolyn R. Wilker is an editor and author from southwestern Ontario. She finds beauty in every season. You'll often see her, camera in hand, taking pictures of things in nature, her grandchildren, friends and family. Many of those photos appear in her blog 'Storygal' where she writes about life, love and gardening.

www.carolynwilker.ca

Lisa Elliott, who wrote our Afterword, is a gifted speaker, and award-winning author of *The Ben Ripple; Choosing to Live through Loss with Purpose* and *Dancing in the Rain; One Family's Journey through Grief and Loss.*

Lisa's passion is sharing the principles and life-giving truths from God's Word straight from the heart. Her writing appears regularly in *Just Between Us* magazine. Other contributions appear in *The Story, Hot Apple Cider with Cinnamon* and in a regular blog for Word Alive Press website. Additionally, she has appeared on Christian television and radio.

A pastor's wife, Lisa and her husband, David, have invested and harvested a fruitful and effective ministry for over thirty years. They have four young adult children (three on earth, one in heaven) one son-in-law, and one grandson.

www.lisaelliottstraightfromtheheart.webs.com
lisakelliott22@gmail.com